The

Millennial

Experience

30 Stories of Hope, Growth and Success

Daniel M. Francis

Port of Spain, Trinidad & Tobago

Published April 15th, 2021

ISBN: 978-0-578-89326-6

DISCLAIMER

Editing: Todd Hunter, Avenue Liteary Services LLC

Author photo courtesy of Josh Rudder, Tova Group

Illustrations courtesy of Desfia Phillips, Uzuridesignedit

Table of Contents

Introduction

The Millennial Experience comes off the heels of my first book *The Millennial Mind: Success Secrets for Unlocking Your Full Potential.* Humbled by the success of *The Millennial Mind* and all the constructive feedback I received, I was moved to share more about the challenges that face Millennials. But this time I decided to do it in a slightly different way. I saw that it was necessary to dive deeper into the numerous situations and circumstances that affect our lives: the Millennial experience.

As you read through the stories you might find that some will speak to you in a meaningful way. You may think to yourself, "Wow, I have gone through this." or "Wow, I am currently going through this." If so, pay careful attention to the solutions proposed. In many cases, the characters make small changes but experience massive and lasting positive change.

This book is part fiction, part non-fiction, and part a mixture of both fiction and non-fiction. The stories are a collection of my personal experiences, experiences of friends, colleagues, and family members. The overarching theme however is hope, growth, and success. We are all experiencing some form of hardship in our lives. Wouldn't it be nice to know that we are not alone in our struggles and even better, to know that there are actions we can take to overcome our challenges?

The stories don't need to be read in any particular order. I wrote this book in hopes of inspiring you to go out and make a change in your life. We all deserve the best that the world has to offer. The catch is that we need to believe that we deserve it and then work at making it a reality.

One last thing: If any of these stories resonate with you, please feel free to share your experience with me at themillennialmind2020@gmail.com. I would love to hear from you.

Thank you for joining in this experience. I hope you enjoy the stories that lie ahead.

Try Guy

Affirmation: I achieve my goals without an ounce of doubt.

"Ben, were you able to hit your target this month?" Everyone in the room turned to Ben in anticipation. They all knew what his response would be. "I tried to get it done but it was too much with all the other work I had on my plate," Ben responded. Ben's manager was furious. Ben hadn't hit his work targets in months and his manager was very close to firing him. Everyone at the meeting was accustomed to Ben's excuses, although according to Ben, he was "trying his best." His response became so typical that he eventually got the name "Try Guy." Always trying but never finishing.

Ben was chewed out by his boss. And yet again, he just appeared fine afterward, disaffected by his boss's disappointment. In his mind, he

—

convinced himself that he tried his best, so if he could not attain the goal, the target was too high. Ben's attitude stood in contrast to his coworkers who typically far exceeded their targets. He arrived back at his cubicle to find that his coworkers had stuck up a small poster on his computer screen. It was a picture of Master Yoda from Star Wars with the words "Do or do not, there is no try" in bold text. Scribbled at the bottom of the page was, "Better get it in gear Try Guy before you get fired." Ben could hear the snickering all around him.

When he arrived home that evening, the words from the Yoda picture were still in his head. He thought, "There is try! I try all the time damn it." He wanted to prove them wrong somehow and decided to sleep on it. The next day when he got to work, he noticed that there was information about the company's 15k run on the notice board. The company had put on this run every year, but Ben never participated. The guys at the office would always make a big fuss about who would finish faster. Ben thought this was his opportunity to prove himself. Ben did a little running back in his school days, although that was a long time ago. He currently was about fifteen pounds heavier than he wanted to be and had a noticeable gut. Yet, he was determined to run.

The first thing he did was Google how to train for a 15k race. There were loads of information that surfaced. He eventually chose a very detailed running regimen that was coupled with a diet plan. Ben was excited! So excited in fact that during the weekend, he bought new running shoes, running shorts, and compression tights." I am all in," he told himself. Day 1 of training required him to run 5km at a comfortable pace. Ben said to himself, "Okay, let's give this a try. . . . I mean I'm gonna get this done!" The slight adjustment in his language felt strange. He hadn't realized how safe he felt including "try" in his sentences. Somehow saying that he would get this done created more pressure, anxiety, and urgency. It was not a comfortable feeling, but he had to get used to it somehow.

His first run was disastrous. He stopped every couple of minutes to take a break and 2kms in, he decided to walk the rest because his body could not take the strain. The run ended terribly but he got it done. Ben created

—

a giant calendar with the days he would run and how many kilometers he'd run on each day. He transferred all the information from the online plan into a more visually pleasing format. Whenever he completed a run, he would place an X over the day. He did this so he could more easily keep track of his progress. He found himself surprised at how satisfying it was tracking his progress and accomplishing little milestones.

Three weeks in and Ben concluded that he really hated running although he kept up with most of his running days. He missed one or two days in between but he felt so bad about it, that he forced himself to run a little more on his next run day. He was now able to run the entire time without stopping. He ran at a slow pace, but it was progress. The healthy diet was also increasing his overall energy levels throughout the day. He decided to use his tracking method for running at his job. He figured it worked for his running so why not try it at work.

He started by setting a target he wanted to achieve weekly. The weekly targets didn't seem as daunting as the monthly targets. He then set mini targets during the day. Every time he hit a target, he would list it as an achievement and congratulate himself. He knew the changes wouldn't be drastic, but he was intent to stick with the mini targets as a bare minimum requirement. While creating the accomplishment sheet at his desk, one of his coworkers walked by and started heckling him. Then the coworker left him by saying, "Try not to work too hard Try Guy." Noticeably annoyed, Ben however came to a realization: he had not used the word "try" in some time. He had become so self-aware that he slowly broke out of the habit of using the word.

About a month later Ben was halfway through his training regimen and the 15k race was fast approaching. He was at another monthly meeting where each employee gave their report. When Ben's manager reached him, there was surprising news. Ben hit his target and surpassed it by 200%. His coworkers all gasped, dumbfounded by the news. "This has to be a joke," they all thought in unison, but it wasn't. Ben was in a zone when it came to reaching his mini targets. He would run out of space to write his mini accomplishments on his sheet because he was doing so well. He gave each step his full attention before moving onto the next as opposed to worrying about steps he had not gotten to yet.

Ben was crushing it at work and his training was going well too. His attitude toward running slowly changed. He still had hate for sore legs, but the running was becoming more enjoyable. With each run he would outperform the last. It became like a game versus himself. Ben was also pleased that his gut was smaller. He no longer felt ashamed in his work shirt.

The day of the race finally arrived, and Ben was ready. His confidence was through the roof as he had transformed from a chubby slacker into a medium built, driven, ball of energy. He was proud of himself and no longer upset that his coworkers placed that picture on his computer that day. It made him realize that he was full of excuses and that he needed to change.

Ben joined the crowds of people at the starting line. One of the officials blew the horn and everyone was off. With a big grin on his face, Ben was out the gates like a thoroughbred racehorse.

***

The words that we use hold immense power. If we use words such as "try," we are admitting that we don't have full control and the lack of accountability will show in our work and our results. You can take control of your life by adding responsibility to your vocabulary. The changes will be subtle at first, but they will begin to show in your actions and behavior. There will be no doubt in your mind that you won't achieve what you say you will. You owe yourself the opportunity to be great. Start with your words and start now.

The Life-Altering List

Affirmation: I create the life I want to live.

Daynah's teachers often described her as bigger than life and destined for greatness such. No pressure, right? Her environment subjected her to a consistent type of pressure, to always be at her best. Not a day went by where she was not reminded of these expectations. Thankfully, she was a hard worker. She was diligent, disciplined, and intelligent—the perfect recipe for success.

Before she even knew what hit her, she was thrown into the tides of the working world. Daynah's career of "choice" was engineering. It was what she thought she was supposed to do. She felt immense pressure pushing forward along the engineering path. She was good at math and physics so it made sense.

When Daynah landed an engineering job, at first it felt new and exciting. Though it was not exactly what she thought it would be like. She expected to know what she was doing but she needed heavy guidance in the beginning. All in all, she felt blessed to have a high-paying job. She knew that many others are not as fortunate so she did not complain. More time went by and the days were blurring into one another. She grew older and acquired more and more responsibilities. She even got a dog, but in the blink of an eye, she began paying a mortgage with her longtime boyfriend.

Life was moving fast and she took the most logical steps. However, an aggravating feeling began to grow within Daynah, more accurately, each morning. A distasteful feeling of resentment. She was ashamed of herself for feeling this way. "How can I feel such an emotion?" she would ask herself. "What an ungrateful person I am," she thought. "People are suffering, struggling to make ends meet each day. Yet, here I am feeling resentful for all I have."

"What right do I have to feel this way?" Daynah asked herself. Yet no answer ever came. She buried the resentment as deeply as she could. "It must stay hidden," she thought. But the experience is still the same daily—the same negative feeling. She felt indignant towards her job. She needed her income to pay the car bill, mortgage, and even for the dog food. She knew her job was merely an avenue for survival.

"Why then do I feel such displeasure?" she wondered. Especially for a career that she invested so heavily in with her time, money, and energy. Daynah got what she wanted yet she hated every minute of being at work. Worse yet, she hated herself for the way she felt. "I am not allowed to feel this way," she said to herself in the mirror daily. "It's all in my head and I am fine," she continued, but was it?

Every so often, she found herself daydreaming of a different life. A life where she woke up each morning excited to start her day. She can't see the work she is doing in the dream clearly but what was apparent was her satisfaction. She saw the passion and drive. There were electricity and vibrancy around her, and she found joy in the little things. Daynah saw glimpses of that life but she could not believe that it was possible. The life she was living was what she chose therefore she felt that had to must stick by it and follow through. If not, then why did she sacrifice so much? She must validate all the work she put in and she must protect the life she built.

One morning Daynah was feeling especially down. She pressed the snooze button five times. She wished she could take a sick day but she knew she had too much work to complete. She had the sudden idea to list all the things about her job that she hated. On her phone, she listed the following:

I hate:
- the constant gossip between co-workers
- that I am penalized for every little mistake
- that I am so tired after work that all I want to do is sleep
- that my boss forces me to do work outside of my job description

- that I feel trapped in this job
- feeling like if I leave then my whole world ends
- the way that some superiors talk down to me like I'm an animal
- that I'm expected to work late without overtime pay

The list continued for pages and pages. She became passionate about all the things she hated but she did not want to stop there. Daynah figured that if this is everything she hated, then her ideal job would be the complete opposite. The idea was a stroke of brilliance. She began writing the opposite of what she hated to see what her perfect job would look like.

I want a job where:
- co-workers respect each other's privacy
- my boss provides constructive feedback when I make mistakes
- I can work from home some days
- I do exactly what I am paid to do
- I don't feel trapped
- I'm encouraged to grow as a person
- there is mutual respect even from superiors

The list of what she wanted was considerably longer than the list of her grievances. When she looked at her list describing the perfect job she felt excited and inspired. She'd never thought about what she'd want from a perfect job. She always believed that you get what you get and that was that. Over the next couple of weeks Daynah began her mornings by reading her perfect job description. She felt supercharged after she read it which motivated her to get up and get to work. Even though things in her job had not changed, she internalized that perfect job description and began to slowly feel emboldened to change her situation.

Daynah made small changes at first. She distanced herself from all the co-workers who engaged in constant gossip. She leveled up by standing her ground when her boss castigated her for a small error she made. Her boss was shocked because Daynah never really spoke up about anything. This sparked a discussion where Daynah vocalized how she felt about different aspects of her role and her grievances. Her boss was mostly unaware of how she felt and together they worked out what could be done differently. The changes weren't drastic but they were a shift in a positive direction. Daynah felt less resentment as the days passed. The trapped feeling dissipated and she felt a rekindling of her excitement for work. This also made her experience greater levels of gratitude for everything in her life. She still read her list every morning before she started her day, excited to do her best.

***

We sometimes feel trapped by our circumstances. We make decisions to the best of our ability and life moves on. It's okay not to feel settled or satisfied with where you are in life. Life is funny like that. You are only genuinely trapped if you accept that you are. If you limit yourself to the four corners of a particular reality, that's the reality you will face. Be brave enough to chase happiness, make changes, and protect and cherish your mental headspace. Vocalize your grievances and start a dialogue about what needs to change. Change in your life will come only when you decide to enact the change you want.

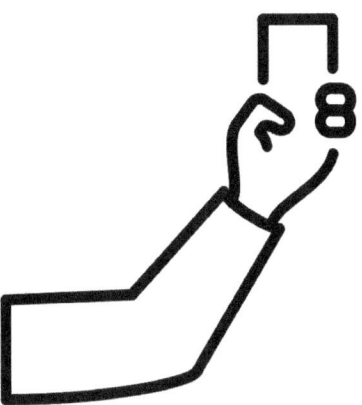

Social Media Dilemma

Affirmation: I am guided by empathy and humility.

Gabrielle let out a big yawn and outstretched her arms above her head. She poked her head out of her covers revealing a disheveled and drowsy face. She then immediately reached for her phone. Like an addict getting their early morning fix, she plugged herself in. She immediately went to the different social media platforms and began scrolling down the newsfeeds. She caught up on all the juicy dramas that she missed while sleeping. Her stomach grumbled loudly. Two hours had passed and she had not left her bed yet. She sat up and scooched to the edge of her bed, still twiddling on her phone, and eventually made her way to the kitchen to prepare breakfast.

Gabrielle had a real addiction. She spent hours on various social media platforms. She could not leave her phone alone for more than twenty minutes. She was obsessed with social media, but she had a following on Instagram, Facebook, and Twitter. By far, however, her favorite platform was Twitter. She loved updating everyone on her life and tweeting fun, quirky, and witty tidbits of information. She would never openly admit it, but she also loved the drama that unfolded on the platform. When someone was having a Twitter beef or someone was being dragged for saying something ludicrous or highly controversial, she would not miss an opportunity to share in the vitriol.

For Gabrielle, social media was more than just entertainment. She knew how to leverage her social media influence and tapped into her large following to grow her online business. She was a boss at organizing launches around her jewelry lines. She made good money every month because she always had so many eyeballs on her social media platforms. So much so that when she had launches of new jewelry lines, typically all the jewelry would sell out in the first week.

One day while scrolling she felt a sudden inspiration and immediately began sketching new jewelry designs. She had created a line of five gorgeous silver necklaces with matching rings. She was proud of what she had imagined and wasted no time producing a new campaign around her new line.

She hyped up the new line for about two weeks. By the time she was ready to drop the new products, her followers were clamoring to buy. When she finally sent out the post unveiling her new jewelry line, her social media platforms exploded expectantly. It was an endless stream of likes, comments, tweets, and retweets. As was the case with her typical launches, her posts would go viral helping her jewelry to sell out in an instant and this launch was no different. By the end of the day, she was sold out. Basking in the splendor of her latest accomplishment, Gabrielle decided to go through more of the retweets of her posts and read all the positive comments. It was then that she saw it.

Someone was claiming that she stole the jewelry design from someone else. Gabrielle was confused. The woman claimed that she recently posted her jewelry line on her page and that Gabrielle had copied her exact pieces. "How insane!?" Gabrielle thought. She immediately sent a reply tweet saying that she didn't copy anyone, and she was annoyed that a "nobody" was trying to tarnish her brand. Nothing was more important to her than the brand she had worked so hard to build. She didn't realize that she had set off a landmine. The girl posted photos of her jewelry line which had dropped before Gabrielle's, and it looked remarkably similar. Not only that but when Gabrielle called the girl "a nobody" it sparked tremendous outrage.

Gabrielle was being called elitist, the hateful 1%, a no-brained influencer, borderline racist among other things. Her reply aggravated the situation and opened up Pandora's box because she was of a lighter complexion and the girl was dark-skinned. "That's not what I meant," she thought. "They are misunderstanding my words; I was upset but I didn't mean anything racist by what I said." However, the damage had been done. Her comments had been retweeted, memed, and shared on other platforms. Anywhere she went on social media, she felt attacked. She had never been on the receiving end of social media vilification. She was having her moment to be dragged through the mud and it was a real mess. Things had escalated quickly, and Gabrielle was becoming overwhelmed. Her attempts to backpedal and explain herself were met with resistance and futility.

To make matters worse there was a call to boycott her business. This was what she feared most. This snowballed into many people who ordered jewelry from the campaign to cancel their orders. Gabrielle was mortified. She felt like her world was collapsing around her. Good friends were messaging her privately criticizing her for her comments. It was brutal. Her inbox was littered with messages. She could not believe how disrespectful people were towards her. She came very close to exploding on many of them, but she restrained herself. Her family members were also attacked. This was her problem, yet expletives were being hurled at her family members on their personal pages. Things were out of hand. She had been on her phone for hours at this point and she began shaking. The whole ordeal had her intensely distressed, so she decided to just unplug from everything by shutting off her phone. She sat in her room and did the only thing she could do, cry.

After a bout of crying and a long useless crusade to save face, Gabrielle was exhausted and fell asleep. She woke up the next morning feeling despondent. She wanted to check her phone but was fearful of what was being said. She didn't much care about what people thought about her, but she feared for the reputation of her business. Those who do not own a business could not imagine how much work goes into building a brand. To see it torn down over one tweet weighed heavily on her. She decided to make breakfast and take a moment to process everything.

She sat silently and thought about everything as she sipped her tea. She thought back to when she got the idea for the jewelry line. "Maybe I had seen her collection while scrolling that day and not even realized it?" she reflected. "I might have not even noticed. Was I the villain in this story?" she questioned. She began realizing that she might have been.

She did not want to evade the elephant in the room anymore, so she put her phone on and immediately posted a heartfelt video putting everything on the table. She apologized for inadvertently copying the woman's jewelry collection and she apologized for her negative comment. She did not attempt to make excuses or pick a fight. She also said that she would discontinue that jewelry line and refund everyone's orders. She knew that her video would not stop the vilification, but she knew that it had to be done. In the past, she had ironically criticized similar apology videos as disingenuous.

As expected, her video was not well received. Some supported her effort and others continued to speak ill of her and her business. She felt powerless to change anyone's perception, so she decided to step away from social media for a bit not only because she was the focus of a lot of hate, but she was mentally depleted. The ordeal made her feel bruised, exposed, mentally depleted, and depressed. She had to protect herself, so she distanced herself from social media for a while.

Throughout her time away from social media, Gabrielle reflected on her entire experience. How painful, terrifying, and denigrating it was. Some of the hateful messages she received still weighed heavily on her mind. She had to constantly remind herself that she was not what others were saying she was. She made a mistake, albeit, a big one. She then thought about the people that she had dragged on social media, whether they had experienced what she was now going through. She never thought about what they felt. "Even if they said something terrible, they are still people with feelings. I think we take things too far on social media," she affirmed.

"It's so crazy how this affects you," Gabrielle thought. She felt worse knowing that she was a part of this toxic culture of dragging people on social media, especially if they posted something that was miscommunicated. Or worse yet, if false information was posted about them and shared. She understood that she made a big mistake. She did not know if her business would be able to recover from the hit. The thought of her business going under made her feel very depressed. It was a vicious cycle. She vowed to never drag anyone on social media again. She also vowed to be careful about what she posted and how she posted it. "You never know who you might hurt and how far the social media community will take things," she thought.

***

Social media can be a double-edged sword. It can be used to accomplish amazing feats but when a mistake is made the backlash can be relentless. A misunderstanding can too easily turn into a good versus evil situation. One side becomes the villain who must be brought to justice. And who knows whether that person's livelihood is being destroyed as a result. The sentiment expressed is that "they must burn." Some become outraged by opinions that they disagree with and the experience turns into a social media shouting match. They inhale the noxious gas emitted from the experience and the social media attack begins to feel like something akin to an old-fashioned torch-wielding riot. Except in this case, it isn't some Frankenstein figure being run out of town, it's a human being who is being attacked.

This is not to say that we should let others off for saying hurtful and downright heinous things on social media but let's not take things too far. Sometimes we are too hasty to jump on the bus when it is time to drag someone's name through the mud. Sometimes we miss the context or simply misunderstand. If everyone begins to vilify an individual and mount an attack too quickly, we never know what our actions will do to that person's mental state. It's easy to vilify someone when we are doing it through our phones, but we must remember that it's still a flesh-and-bones person on the receiving end.

Do It All Chris

Affirmation: I am worthy of life and all its beautiful blessings.

Trigger Warning: This story contains triggering content on suicide.

"Chris you are the man," cheered his coworkers. Chris had done it again. He solved a problem that no one else in the office was able to figure out. He once again was being praised for an accomplishment, an almost weekly occurrence at work . . . and something he'd grown accustomed to throughout his life.

Chris was what some would consider a high school star. He played on his school's football team and his talent afforded him a starting position as a young student. He was before his time. He got the nickname "Do It All Chris" from his ability to strike the ball like the best of them but

———

he could also play any position on the field, even goalie. Nevertheless, the nickname stuck.

As a footballer, Chris never got distracted when it came to his schoolwork. He always scored within the top ten in his class. Even when his family came upon tough times immediately after he graduated, he took it upon himself to get a job to help out. He had to put aside a few dreams as his family came first.

With an early introduction into the world of work, he grew accustomed to the ins and outs of office life. He had his main job as a sales rep, which he executed with the kind of panache and geniality that made him not only lovable but the top salesperson in the company for two years running. Yet he always made the time to help his coworkers with the little things. He lived for the applause. Not much had changed from those school days while on the football field.

Do It All Chris was riding a wave of satisfaction that never seemed to crash. His relationship with his girlfriend was also going well. They recently moved in together and he consistently showered her with gifts. "Life is good," he would think to himself.

One day Chris was meeting with a manager from a company that he was pursuing for a sale. The guy loved his energy and asked him if he would be interested in working for their company. Chris did not know what to think. He loved his current employer and it was the only company he had worked for since leaving school. Not only that, but his coworkers were also like his family. The manager could sense Chris's reluctance, so he wrote something on a piece of paper. "These are the benefits and the salary," and slid the piece of paper over to Chris. The salary blew Chris away. Chris would get a company car in addition to everything else. The thought of being able to upgrade his life and not having to use public transportation anymore made him noticeably excited. The manager knew that Chris was sold.

Chris gave his two weeks' notice and broke the news to his coworkers. They were devastated but happy for him. They carried out a heartfelt last day of work for him. Chris began second-guessing his decision to leave but ultimately it was time for bigger and better things.

Chris entered his new office with all the excitement of a kid in a toy store; excited for what he would see and do. The layout of the floor was different from what he was used to. His desk was isolated from the other desks. He also noticed that there weren't many people in the office. He reasoned that everyone was out making sales as this company was heavy on salespersons. He settled in and got to work.

The first couple of weeks were a bit bumpy. To him, the products Chris was expected to sell were gimmicky and low quality. However, he had a job to do. Maybe it was his lack of faith in the product or the fact that they gave him a strict sales script to stick to, but he was off his normal game. He had a lot more freedom to do what he wanted in his last job. One day his manager stormed into his office and screamed at him. Chris was not keeping up to date with the email memos and had given numerous clients wrong information about the products. He was not used to this type of behavior and it caught him off guard. Chris was not one to check his email often and he was slowly realizing that his carefree way of doing things would not work in this new environment.

Chris began to buckle down and operate within the guidelines the company had set up. Chris found that even after working a full day, he was not producing the sales he needed. He found himself scrambling, as his salary was based mostly on commissions. He began working longer hours to compensate and spending less time on the things he loved. The pressure was mounting and it was all made worse by his manager's tendency to scream at him.

Chris had not hit his target for two months in a row and, as a result, some of his pay was deducted. This frustrated Chris to no end because he had moved to a more expensive apartment complex. Since taking the new job, his expenses had increased so he could not afford to make less on any given month. He regularly left home before the sunrise and returned in the dark of night. He would barely see his girlfriend during the day and had begun leaving little love notes around the house to show that he still cared.

One Sunday afternoon he found himself working as always but at least he was home. The pressure was on to hit his monthly target which he was still quite far from reaching. The thought of not hitting his target caused a cascade of negative thoughts and emotions. The reprehension that would come from his manager, the look on his girlfriend's face, and the disappointment he would feel for not providing, all weighed heavily on him. It was in that moment of fear and doubt that Chris recalled an odd memory. He remembered his schoolmate who had committed suicide two years prior. "Why did that memory pop into my mind?" he wondered. He paid it no mind and went back to work.

A few weeks later, Chris was growing more depressed by the day. He was caught in an endless cycle of work and disappointment. To make matters worse, the thoughts of his friend who had killed himself kept surfacing in his mind. The more he tried to ignore it, the more he thought about it. He began wondering why his friend did it and how he must have felt before taking his life. He acknowledged that the thoughts he was having were dangerous. His girlfriend was also noticing the change in him and she knew it was not only the pressure of work but that it was something more. She was worried about the person that he was becoming. She cornered him one morning before he could leave for work and pressed him on what was happening. She missed her boyfriend and all the time that they would spend together. Chris could not help himself; tears began streaming down his face and he revealed all the pressure and terrifying thoughts he was having.

It took a considerable amount of effort for Chris to open up in therapy and start feeling better. After five months of therapy, he was beginning to see some semblance of a light at the end of the tunnel. Some major changes were made after that emotional exchange with his girlfriend. He decided to quit his job and find another job. They moved out of their apartment and found a more affordable one. His girlfriend handled the expenses as he began therapy. She told him not to worry about anything besides getting better. Chris hated the idea of speaking to someone about his problems. It was his pride. He felt weak and ashamed for reaching this point.

It took a while for him to realize that his views on therapy needed to change for it to work. He had an excellent therapist who was patient with him. She never rushed him. After some time, he was able to express difficult emotions and be more open to the process. It was by no means a quick process. He was not out of the woods, but he felt comfortable enough to begin looking for work again. "Do It All Chris is making a comeback," he said to himself with a slight smile.

***

We sometimes create these mental cages and place ourselves inside of them. And we can't see a way out of the cage. The environment that we're in and the negative thoughts about it shower more and more darkness onto us until we can't see. When this happens, extend your hand to receive help. Do not allow yourself to be consumed by the darkness, by the depression. There are people out there who care about you deeply and they want to see you happy and alive. Put pride, doubt, and anxiety aside and get the help you need. Your mental health is no joke. You deserve to live your life with you in control.

Supporting Resource

T&T Suicide Hotline: 1 800 SUICIDE/ 1 800 273 TALK(8255)

An Overthinker's Report

Affirmation: I tackle life's obstacles and inch closer and closer to success.

"Thanks for listening attentively everyone. If you have any questions, feel free to come to my office so we can work through them. Stefan, since you are new here you can work with Antonio for the time being. We have a heavy workload this quarter but it's nothing that we can't handle. Stay focused everyone," Gail said. Stefan marveled at Gail's confidence to lead. It was only his first week, but he felt like an effective part of the team thanks to her clear communication.

"Some people are just born great. All that confidence. She's also so organized even though she is leading such a big team," Stefan said about Gail as Antonio began showing him his task. Antonio replied,

"Yea, that's our Gail. But you'd be surprised to know that she was a real wreck in the past." Stefan raised his eyebrows to express disbelief. "Yea she was pretty timid and something as simple as communicating information in front of other people would be problematic for her." Stefan could not believe it. "She would freeze up, take long pauses, and trip over her words. I don't know what changed but whatever it was had a huge impact. Anyways, pay attention," said Antonio as he continued to show Stefan how to do the task.

Stefan knocked on Gail's door and entered timidly. "Hi Stefan, what can I help you with?" Shyly, Stefan asked, "I want to put my best foot forward as I am new. I tend to overthink when I am nervous and I am new here so I feel especially nervous. I was wondering if you had any advice?" Gail smiled and said, "Have a seat. Let me give you these four steps that worked well for me."

four years ago

Gail stood in front of everyone holding the report. She had double-checked and even triple-checked the information before the meeting, yet she hesitated to give the results. She was prepared to speak but a thought struck her; what if I made a mistake. That thought stopped her cold in her tracks. She began going through the results of the report again and again in her head. She refused to make a fool of herself like the last time she was tasked with giving a report. She won't ever forget that last time. She pronounced the word "necessary" incorrectly and she reported some figures that weren't accurate. A flood of shame washed

---

34

over her as she recalled the memory. She felt like she let her team down that day because of her performance.

While her internal dialogue was rattling on, Gail had not said a word and was mumbling to herself. Everyone waited impatiently for her to simply read her report. The moans of annoyance became noticeable, snapping Gail out of her thoughts. She began reading her report. She stumbled here and there and rushed through parts of it. It was clear she wanted to get it done as quickly as possible. After the meeting her team members told her to take it easy next time. "You need to stop overthinking it so much. You did a good job leading us this month," they said. But Gail felt otherwise. The only thing on her mind was all the little things she didn't do well. Topping that list was the poor showing she put on minutes earlier when all she had to do was communicate the reports to everyone.

Gail was a chronic overthinker. She could not help herself. She analyzed and overanalyzed constantly. She desperately wanted to become a manager someday and she had great potential but her tendency to overthink had put a huge wrench in her hopes. She would overthink so much that it would lead to her procrastinating simple tasks that should have taken her five to ten minutes. That night as she lay in bed recounting the day's activities, she found herself unable to sleep. This was nothing new. She would often be unable to sleep because her brain was on overdrive. Thinking about her mistakes or even what a coworker meant when they said something in a particular manner. It was all in her head. For Gail, overthinking things had become exhausting.

Aware of her condition, she decided to look up how to stop overthinking since she was going to be up anyway. She found an article online about habits that drain your energy. The main focus of the article was how to combat overthinking. She thought she hit the jackpot. Just two minutes into the article, she was triggered by what she read. The words were almost attacking her. It spoke about all the wasted energy that goes into overthinking and how it affects your self-esteem. It was something she knew all too well. The article even spoke about how overthinking can negatively affect your sleep. She thought about how ironic this was as she was up late that night because of her active brain.

The article laid the solution out simply. It said that when you begin overthinking you need to stop, acknowledge that you are overthinking, note that you are doing a great job, and focus on the bigger picture. It sounded simple enough. She had nothing to lose and decided to try it every time she felt the urge to overthink. The next day at work she wrote down the steps she needed to follow when the urge to overthink hit her. It was written on her phone so that she could easily glance at it if needed. Every time she felt like she was about to overthink something, she peeked at the note.

Several times during the day she would glance at the note. At first, she thought the instructions were having little effect, but she knew that it was something new and it would take time. She would not give up so easily. She saw her coworkers chuckle after she walked by and began thinking that they were somehow laughing at her then she immediately looked at her note. When her boss ended a conversation abruptly, she began to think that maybe she did something wrong, but she immediately looked at her note. Even when she wasn't overthinking, she would take a peek at the note. It just made her feel calm and focused.

A month later after religiously following the instructions from the article, Gail did not need the note anymore. She looked at it so much over the course of that month that she had it memorized. When she felt the urge to overthink, she would mentally re-focus herself.

The time had come again for her to give her report. She stood up confidently. She looked down at the report and felt a slight surge of fear. She was afraid that she would revert to her old overthinking ways. She closed her eyes and mentally went through her steps: stop, acknowledge that you are overthinking, note that you are doing a great job, and focus on the bigger picture. She opened her eyes and read the report with confidence. Her coworkers were shocked. They began wondering who this changed person in front of them.

"Stop, acknowledge that you are overthinking, note that you are doing a great job, and focus on the bigger picture. Write it somewhere where you will see it when you feel yourself overthinking. Make it a game and develop it into a habit. I promise you it will help you," Gail said with a warm smile to Stefan. He thanked her and left her office excited to give this new advice a try.

***

Overthinking can hold you back from being your best. It's a habit and as such, you can create a new one to overwrite it. Follow the process that Gail did: stop, acknowledge that you are overthinking, note that you are doing a great job, and focus on the bigger picture. Repetition is your friend here. The more you remind yourself to follow the process the quicker it will become a habit and replace your bad habit of overthinking. Keep focused as you work on building a better you.

Parkinson's Law

Affirmation: I invest in my greatest asset: myself.

"Why oh why is there never enough money to do things," Akash retorted. "No matter the month I always feel like I am just barely over broke. This is exhausting." Akash was blessed that he was able to make good money. But as his income increased so did his spending. He needed a car and he moved out of his parent's house and began renting. "Who knew being a responsible adult would be so taxing . . . literally. As soon as I get the money it leaves my account. So many bills, and insurance payments to boot. When I leave the office, all I want to do is spend the little I have left in the day to forget my worries," he complained.

Living paycheck to paycheck was becoming exhausting. When the money for bills left his account each month, it felt like he was being stabbed in the chest. Yet, every month was the same. Work, work, work, then pay bills. Any money left over he would spend on partying or drinking with the boys. There needed to be some relief he rationalized. His friends were in no better situation than him. They all had similar feelings and grievances. One day while out getting lunch he saw that the lottery jackpot was now at five million dollars. He began fantasizing about all the things he could do with that money. He saw himself lazing on a beach in Jamaica with a Mai Tai in both hands. He saw himself on a yacht sailing across the ocean with the arms of a beautiful woman draped around his neck. Before he knew it, he was in line ready to buy a few tickets.

He spent the rest of the day fantasizing about what he would do if he won that money. The dreams became more extravagant as the day went on. His daydreaming was interrupted by a coworker reminding him of the mandatory seminar that was about to start. Ironically, the topic was financial literacy. Everyone in the office gathered and listened as the financial advisor began pouring on the advice. Akash, still caught in his daydreams, did not catch much of what was being said. He did, however, zone in when he heard the advisor say this:

"You could win the lottery today and it could be the worst thing to happen to you if you are not financially literate. Having more money exacerbates your negative traits and the money can disappear as quickly as it comes. You've heard the saying, more money, more problems. Well, the reality is that the majority of people don't know what to do with their money when they have it. Also, when they get more money, their expenses tend to rise in lockstep with their earnings. This is a well-known theory called Parkinson's Law."

The advisor's words seemed eerily familiar to Akash. His expenses had increased as his income increased but he thought that was to be expected. "I worked hard for my money and I deserve to upgrade my life a little," he thought. The seminar ended and everyone went back to their work. Akash was a bit annoyed but eventually he returned to his daydreaming. After work, Akash went out for a few drinks with some coworkers. They drank away their problems and complained about how life was setting them up to be poor. A typical conversation for them. He got home later that night drunk and unsteady. He threw off his clothes and dove into his bed. His lottery tickets scattered all over the floor when he threw his pants on the ground and the last thought he had was how different his life would be if he only won the lottery.

Akash woke up around noon the next day. Hungover and with a terrible headache, he dragged himself out of bed to make a cup of coffee. The lottery tickets were still draped across the floor, so he picked them up and looked online to see what numbers were called. Akash pressed the mug against his lip and took a sip. He immediately sprayed his coffee all over the counter and computer screen as he stood dumbfounded. One of his tickets matched! He was now a millionaire! He jumped up in the excitement and began screaming and dancing. "My life begins from today!" he screamed.

With the money secured, it was time to spend. Akash bought a new home and two new cars. He made sure to post it on social media to make all his friends and coworkers jealous. Speaking of work, he never went back to his job. He called and let them know that millionaires don't work a job and hung up. He called all of his friends over to his new place and had a huge party. It was wild but that was only the beginning. It was time to get that yacht he had always dreamed about. He chose one that looked as close to the one he had envisioned. Every weekend, he went out on his new boat with different groups of friends. It was a dream.

He enjoyed the best foods and frequently took trips to different destinations he had always dreamed about visiting. On his most recent trip, he took his new girlfriend to Paris where they enjoyed all the best accommodations. In the blink of an eye, two years had passed. It all happened so quickly. Akash woke up fully content with life and excited to enjoy it even more. He pulled out his laptop to plan his next big trip. He heard Australia was a big adventurous place so decided to go there. He pulled up the flights and booked one right on the spot or attempted to. The payment would not go through. Confused by this, Akash opened his online banking to check his accounts. All the blood drained right out of his face as he looked on in disbelief. His account was empty. "How could this have happened!?" he thought.

With no money in the bank, there was no way he could maintain some of the many expensive things he bought. He could no longer afford the lavish vacations and parties. His girlfriend eventually left him and his friends disappeared one by one. He hadn't put any of his money away anywhere, so he had to sell what he had to survive.

Akash couldn't imagine going back to his old life. He grimaced at the thought of crawling back to his old job and begging them to take him back. His pride would not allow it but what other options did he have? "How did it come to this?" he questioned. In that instance, the words of the financial advisor popped into his head, "Having more money exacerbates your negative traits and the money can disappear as quickly as it comes." He began resenting all the money he spent. He realized he hadn't changed. He hated to admit it, but the advisor was right.

Akash woke up in a cold sweat. Dazed and confused, head pounding. He sat on the edge of his bed and planted his feet on the ground, looked down, and saw lottery tickets scattered all over the ground. "It was all a dream . . ." he realized. He laughed out loud in relief. Now he knew his problem was not money but his lifestyle and his way of thinking. He needed to get his life in some type of order. He messaged one of his coworkers to get the number for the financial advisor who held the seminar. He immediately called him to set up a meeting. The thought crossed his mind to throw out the lottery tickets and begin making breakfast. "Who am I kidding," he said. He was too curious. He pulled up the video to see if he had won. "It was still a chance at millions of dollars," he chuckled.

***

The more knowledge we equip ourselves with, the better our decision-making. This rings true especially thinking about financial literacy. The average person wants more money but rarely knows how to manage it. However, when a person is financially literate, they could lose all their money and resurrect their wealth in no time because they have the knowledge-base and experience. Try to be aware of any personal habits that can impact your ability to build wealth. Take the time to learn how money works. And know that when you invest in yourself, it's the greatest investment you can make.

How do you visualize your success?

Affirmation: I achieve whatever I put my mind to.

The "New Year, new me" posts had begun and Martin could not stop rolling his eyes in irritation as he scrolled through social media. "Yes, Stephanie, it is a new year but you are still the same," he joked to himself as he read Stephanie's post about her New Year's resolutions. Martin hated the days leading up to the new year and the following month. He found that people around him and on social media fooled themselves with this renewed sense of being. To him, nothing had changed besides the calendar. He noticed that people would set goals, and after a few weeks, they would begrudgingly give up on the goals.

—

Yet, once the new year came around again, they would engage in this sadistic ritual all over again.

Martin felt above it all, but he was once just like the people he criticized. At the beginning of each new year, he would set goals but each year the same thing happened. He would never follow through and then get annoyed with himself for trying. So, he stopped creating new year resolutions and goals altogether. What was the point?

While scrolling on his newsfeed he came upon an interesting post. It asked a simple question: "How do you visualize your success?" Martin was intrigued by the question because it was different. It did not ask about goals. Rather it encouraged him to consider what he wanted out of life.

"What a simple exercise," he thought. "Success means living in a big house. Making plenty of money. Enjoying a happy life with family and friends." Martin visualized the outside of a big red mansion, a huge pile of money, and relishing in a few laughs with some friends and family. The exercise seemed too easy but then he read the caption:

"Visualizing success can seem like a simple task, but when imagining the life you want or the things you want to have, it is best to be specific about it. Visualization can be a powerful tool if it's done correctly. When doing this exercise, be specific about what you see, how you feel, and lay out all the extraneous details."

After reading the caption, Martin felt embarrassed because his vision for success seemed overly vague. He tried the exercise again and attempted to be more specific. He focused on the home he wanted, the one he had always dreamed about. He knew he wanted to live in a big mansion, but he never took the time to think about the interior. He began in the bedroom and imagined a big king-sized bed with white sheets and a fairly large room with a large walk-in closet filled with clothes and shoes. He paused for a bit realizing that he should also imagine women's clothing as he would be sharing his home with his wife. He then added a section in the walk-in closet with his wife's clothes.

He continued on to the different areas of his bedroom from the lavish white tiled bathroom to the balcony overlooking the garden below. He was having fun with it all but conceded that the task was pretty difficult. He was struggling to see some sections of the bedroom and there was still the rest of the mansion. An exercise that seemed easy at first glance was now becoming more difficult. It was clear that he had grown accustomed to defining success with vague ideas of what he wanted. He needed to re-work his vision for his future.

The outlook seemed grim. He didn't have a specific idea of what he wanted in most areas of his life. "How did I not notice this?" he thought. His mind then drifted back to the New Years' resolution posts. "Maybe those posts pissed me off so much because I rarely achieve my own goals. It's pretty clear now why I don't. I don't even know exactly what I want!" he asserted. This realization bothered him deeply. He became enraged because he believed that he had been wasting so much of his life drifting aimlessly.

He calmed himself and decided to do the visualization exercise every day. Each day he would spend twenty minutes focusing on a specific area of his life. When he began this daily habit certain areas of his life were very difficult to visualize. Thinking about his spiritual life, he could not visualize anything outside of going to church on Sundays and praying each morning. Other areas were easier. When he visualized his dream job, although he could not tell what job he held, he did, however, see how long he worked, how he felt while working, and how much money he made.

After a few days Martin began writing down what he saw in his visualizations. He would forget specific details if he didn't put them on paper. At times throughout the day, he would sneak a peek at what he wrote. Reading the visualizations made him feel more confident and motivated to do his day-to-day work because he felt like he was now moving towards a higher purpose. Seeing his goals written out confirmed for him that his daily actions were leading him to what he wanted out of life.

The change in Martin was gradual but considerably effective. Martin went from being complacent and wayward to goal-oriented and hyper-focused on his future. By visualizing on a daily basis, he felt like he was halfway to achieving his goals. He was continually shocked that a simple exercise could make him feel so confident. He could see how the trajectory of his life could change for the better. All he needed to do now was put in the work.

***

If you can create a mental environment where you already feel like you have achieved your goals, then you are already one step closer to achieving them. You will be more confident, focused, and driven when executing your day-to-day activities. Life can be so much more rewarding when you know that the actions you are taking daily are leading you exactly where you want to go. You only need to pick a destination and visualizing will help you drop that location pin.

When visualizing, find a method that works best for you. Whether you are writing it out or keeping it in your mind, be sure to be as specific as possible. No detail is too extraneous. The more specific you are, the more purposeful your goals and actions will be. Be patient when developing a habit of visualization. At first, it may feel strange to close your eyes and use your imagination. And it may not feel like it's working. But bear with it. You will eventually move past those feelings and begin focusing on what success looks and feels like to you. Take this step into creating a future you want for yourself.

The Blame Game

Affirmation: I make no excuses and strive for greatness each day.

"Next! Can I have your order, sir?" asked Jessica. The customer looked up and began scanning the menu. Jessica became immediately annoyed. "So, he couldn't look at the menu while he was waiting in the line!?" she thought to herself as she made an irritated face. The customer noticed her annoyance and quickly gave their order, paid, and hustled off to the side. "If only my parents made good money to send me to a good school. Then I would have a better education and wouldn't be working at this dump," she thought to herself. She remembered how the rich kids got to go to expensive after-school classes and they always did so much better than her. She resented them for their progress.

It was finally closing time and the manager called Jessica aside to speak to her. He explained that customers were complaining about her attitude at the cash register. "This was the fourth complaint this week Jessica. Anymore and I will be forced to let you go," he warned. Jessica grumbled. "If you guys spent money to train us properly maybe I'd do a better job," she mumbled. Her manager did not hear what she said and that was probably for the best. Her mood which was already lousy had worsened considerably. However, she took solace in knowing that tomorrow was Saturday and the only work she had to do was a three-hour promotional gig for a popular milk drink brand. "Easy money," she thought.

The next day, Jessica pulled up to the supermarket ready to do the job. The person who organized the promotional work was flushed with anger when she saw Jessica. "Why are you late?" she growled. "There was a lot of traffic on the way here and I did not know where the grocery was exactly, but I am here now," Jessica replied. The organizer was not entertained by her excuses and told her that her pay would be cut because of her lateness. Jessica was furious at her response. She needed the extra money and she felt it was not her fault that she was late.

She stood in the aisle of the supermarket noticeably irate with the product samples in her hands. She couldn't stop thinking about how she would be making less than promised and how unfair it all was. Caught up in her thoughts she ignored shoppers as they walked through the aisles. She was supposed to be engaging them about the product and giving away samples, but she couldn't be bothered. Realizing that she had not been doing her job and time was almost up, she began handing out samples to anyone nearby. She even forced the samples on the cashiers and employees in the back rooms.

She dumped the rest of the products in a nearby trash can and headed home. She was met with a scathing message from the organizer accusing her of giving out the samples to the employees at the supermarket as opposed to the customers. The message went on and on about how selfish and unbelievable Jessica's actions were and that not only would she not be paid but she wouldn't be used again. Jessica was furious. She replied with a long message saying that the product was terrible anyway and it was not her fault that no one wanted to buy it. "Now I've wasted hours of my Saturday and I have nothing to show for it," she complained.

Jessica decided to drown her sorrows by binge-watching a TV series. Hours into her binge marathon she received a message from her close friend Candyce saying that she was outside. Jessica was in no mood for any company, but her friend was already there, so she got up and went to the door. She let Candyce in and they sat to talk. "I heard you and the organizer had a big falling out today. I was surprised to hear that. What happened?" asked Candyce. "They wanted me to give out samples of a terrible milk drink that nobody wanted and they didn't even pay me for my time! I should sue them," Jessica said angrily.

"We both know that isn't the case. Jessica when are you going to start being real with yourself?" Candyce asked. Jessica was puzzled. She angrily squinted her eyes at Candyce and shook her head indicating that she did not know what Candyce meant. Candyce continued, "We grew up together and we've both had it pretty rough but when are you going to stop blaming everything and everyone for every misgiving in your life? I vouched for you so that you could get that promotional gig and because of what you did I also look bad. Take some accountability for your actions and your life. As a friend, it's hard to see you living your life this way." Jessica felt ambushed. "Don't act like you know me. You don't know anything about me so don't speak about my experiences. Get out!" Candyce quickly left but before she did, she said, "Just think about what I said okay." Jessica slammed the door behind Candyce.

"The nerve of that woman!" Jessica exclaimed. "Telling me what I should and shouldn't do!" Jessica could not calm down. An already turbulent day was ending on an even worse note. She wanted to think of anything else so she continued watching her show and eventually fell asleep. Sunday flew by in an instant and it was almost Monday. Jessica dreaded having to go to work and could already feel herself getting very negative. Worst of all she was still thinking about what Candyce said. It drove her up a wall that she could not expel Candyce's words out of her mind. She kept thinking that things were not her fault and hated that no one else could see it.

Monday morning and she was working at the cash register as usual. She was in no mood and could see the watchful eye of her manager analyzing everything that she did. As much as she hated the job, she had to admit that she needed it. Something had to change or she would be fired. She decided to heed Candyce's advice, no matter how much it annoyed her to do so. She would try to be more accountable for her actions and not pass blame. As she took the orders that day, the same customer who she had been rude to last week was in the line once again. She took it upon herself to apologize for her rude behavior the week before. The customer smiled and placed the order.

Jessica felt like crap after that. She hated admitting that she did something wrong. It made her feel weak and she hated every minute of it. "If this is what I am supposed to be doing, I don't see how this will help me," she thought to herself. After work, she decided to call the organizer from the promotional gig and apologize for her behavior. She had to admit that the money from the gigs came in handy and it was worth trying to repair the relationship. Still, it took her an hour to psyche herself up to do it. When she finally made the call, she was honest about what she did and she apologized profusely. She told her that she was not expecting to get the opportunity to work with them again, but she was grateful for the opportunity that was given.

Again, it pained her heavily to admit to her failures. She felt lesser than and hated every minute of it. The organizer was still furious at Jessica but accepted the apology and said that she would consider taking her back in the future. "At least something good may come from all this," she thought. Jessica had to admit to herself that although it was frustrating to admit that she was the reason that things were going wrong in her life, she felt strangely motivated to do something about it.

Jessica began thinking about how she could change. Now that she wasn't so focused on the people and circumstances she felt were to blame for her current situation, she could start seeing some possible paths to change. She decided to return to school. She took evening classes in hopes of getting better qualifications and ultimately a better job. She tried work and school before, but she constantly complained about the workload, the hours spent in class, and the teachers that taught too quickly for her to keep up.

It was time for her to stop blaming her parents for her lack of progress. "I am a big woman now and although things weren't perfect for me growing up, I have to decide what happens to me now," Jessica declared. She was tired of being stuck and she desperately wanted the change. She made small changes but she was confident that eventually she would start seeing the changes she wanted to see. A little progress is still progress.

***

It's so easy to pass blame. You can blame your parents, your past, and your circumstances. The truth is that we are all not dealt a fair hand. Some have it harder or easier than others. However, at some point it is in your best interest to accept the hand you were dealt in life and take responsibility for steering your life in the desired direction. Yes, what's happened in your past has some influence on your journey but there comes a point where you need to take responsibility for your actions and your life. When you clear out negative habits like complaining and passing blame, you open wide the door of possibilities. You become wholly focused on what you must do to better yourself. True empowerment is equipping yourself with the belief that you are accountable for yourself. You choose what you do, when you do it, and make no excuses.

Boomers vs. Millennials

Affirmation: I am enough.

Janel: "Entitled, impatient, poor planning just to name a few. Plain talk bad manners. I see it in most of y'all."

Michael: "That is not fair and your generation can only see things from your perspective. You have no idea what we are going through."

What started as a small complaint about Millennials exploded into a full-on debate about one generation versus the other.

Michael: "It's so easy to drop these blanket terms on us Millennials but we aren't the way we are by accident. We are a product of our upbringing and environment. And before you forget, we are a product of your generation."

Janel: "So it's our fault that y'all can't cope? Take responsibility for yourself. Are you all not adults?"

Michael was getting noticeably frustrated because he wanted his superior to understand where he, and by extension, his generation was coming from.

Michael: "Yes, we are responsible for ourselves, but your generation sure doesn't take it easy on us. Let's break it down. You say we are entitled but we don't know any better. Our entire school career we are fed this belief that if we get a good education, we would be set with a good job when we leave school."

Janel: "Yea, just like in my generation all you need to do is get a good education, get a job, work hard, and you are set."

Michael: "But that isn't the case. First of all, your generation and my generation are very different. There are more people with degrees in my generation than in yours. A degree isn't anything worth praising in today's society. We now need more to distinguish ourselves in the job market."

Janel: "Okay, I can agree there. There is a difference there but those that do have jobs stay home and freeload off of their parents for way longer than they should. I see that as poor planning for your future and outright laziness."

Michael: "Is it only poor planning or is there more at play here? When my parents were my age they were already married with three kids. At a point, my mother was the only one working and she was able to handle payments on a car, rent, and regular expenses. That is impossible for me on the salary I'm making. Millennials make much less than Boomers did at the same age."

Michael pulled out his phone and did a quick Google search.

Michael: "Look."

Michael gestured at his phone's screen.

Michael: "It says here that Millennials make 20% less than Boomers did at the same stage of life. I'm not just making this up. To add to that, some of us are having quarter-life crises. We expect that we would be so much further ahead in life. We thought we would have moved out by now, found that dream job, or maybe be married with kids but we were not prepared for this constant disappointment and pressure because we aren't where we want to be."

Janel: "Hmmm…maybe that wouldn't be such a problem if you stayed employed at a company for more than a year or two. I've been working here for almost fifteen years and I've worked my way up the ladder and increased my income steadily. Y'all don't have the patience and want the reward now and that's not how the real-world works."

Michael: "I would admit we lack patience, but we grew up with technology. We are so used to instant access to everything and it's just how we are wired. We are more fast-paced and we believe we deserve more. How are we expected to stay at a company where we see little opportunity to move up while we make barely enough money to do anything with? We also want to feel like what we are doing matters. With some companies, we are stuck doing monotonous tasks that make us feel like our roles aren't important. I know I am simply a trainee currently but I would want to know that what I do is making a difference in some way. If I don't think what I do matters, my heart won't be in the work. It will just be a job."

Janel rolled her eyes and threw her hands up in the air dramatically.

Janel: "Come on now. You are living a fantasy. Life doesn't always play out that way. You sometimes need to start with the grunt work to set the foundation for a better life in the future. At least you have a job. Better to be working without the fulfillment you are talking about than to be jobless and struggling."

Michael: "Maybe, but for most of us we would eventually disconnect and want to find a job that can make us feel fulfilled or the very least make us feel like we are part of something bigger. We know we should be grateful for what we have because some don't have anything but deep down it still feels like we could and should be doing better. It also doesn't help that we are patronized so heavily. When we question a procedure or come with any new ideas, it lands on deaf ears or is met with immediate resistance."

Janel: "Well, I don't know what to tell you there. You can't expect companies to change or consider everything you say. It's a business at the end of the day."

Michael: "Well, you can't expect us to be satisfied with working in a place that does not fulfill our needs and wants. We aren't the same as your generation. I just think the hate and prejudice towards Millennials need to stop. We are made out to be this horrible generation of people that seemed to be blamed for everything, yet we are driving innovation everywhere we go. Yes, we have our challenges, we all do, but we have our value and we have so much to give."

There was a brief silence as both sides digested what was said and they all eventually got up and shuffled back to their desk to finish the day's work.

***

There are some negative stigmas attached to Millennials. We are not the entitled creatures that we are sometimes made out to be. There are reasons behind our behavior. Those who misunderstand us may need to have the kind of conversation—like Michael and Janel's—that will allow them to see the world from our perspective. The truth is that each generation, in many ways, is influenced by social and cultural factors, and they are products of the generation that came before. The baton of power will eventually be passed to Millennials who we will have to steer the ship eventually. The trials that we confront and challenges that we overcome are just preparation for that reality.

Self-Help Books . . . Genuine or Fraud?

Affirmation: I am a life-long learner.

Two more pages left and Jeremiah was grinning from ear to ear. He was almost done reading *The Seven Habits of Highly Successful People*. "What a great book?!", he said aloud. This was his tenth self-help book in two months. A personal record for him. He thrived on reading these books. He was what you would call a serial self-help book reader. His girlfriend would tell him it was like an addiction. But for Jeremiah, it was a great addiction to have!

He was barely reading at all a few months earlier. Thanks to his girlfriend that all changed. Jeremiah was obsessed with becoming a

CEO for as long as he could remember. It had been his dream ever since he was a young boy. He found leadership alluring. However, Jeremiah never felt like he was any closer to becoming a CEO. He worked as a customer service representative. A position at the very bottom of the organization and his chances for moving up in the organization seemed small.

Jeremiah's girlfriend was a bookworm. She loved finding a quiet spot to get lost in one of her romance novels. She could devour an entire novel in half a day. Jeremiah would constantly disturb her during her reading time. One day she decided to do something about it. She came across a snippet of information that outlined that the typical CEO reads 50-60 books per year and an idea was hatched. She told Jeremiah this information and convinced him to join her during her reading time instead of disturbing her. As much as he protested the idea of reading that many books, he was very much motivated to become a CEO and so he began his reading journey.

At first, he only read for ten minutes a day as that was all he could handle with his short attention span. Even for that short space of time, he fidgeted constantly and checked his phone every few minutes. Eventually, after a few days, he grew accustomed to his pre-scheduled reading time and increased it to thirty minutes a day and then to an hour. He even kept notes in a special notebook. He loved the idea that he was getting that much closer to reaching "CEO level" of learning. He even joined a book club and a few reading groups that were recommending great self-help books.

Jeremiah would keep a list of all the books he read plastered on the wall of his room. He had a goal of reading 50-60 books for the year.

He felt a rush of accomplishment after turning the final page of the book he was reading. He turned to his girlfriend overflowing with excitement and attempted to make eye contact. She tried to ignore him because she was still enjoying her book. "Babe another one done!" Jeremiah bragged. She turned to him coolly and said, "Great babe . . . now let me finish mine, please." Her reading time was now filled with his incessant talking. Her master plan had taken an unexpected turn and somehow made her situation worse.

Jeremiah, still speaking to his girlfriend, announced, "I'm ready to jump into the next one." He hadn't grasped how inconsiderate his actions were. She was understandably confused. "How could someone who reads so many self-help books not experience any positive change in their life," she thought to herself. Yet when she asked him what new information he learned, he never had a satisfactory answer. It was as though he hadn't retained much of what he read. It was as if the accomplishment of finishing the book was worth more to Jeremiah than digesting and implementing the information. "What was the point?" she thought.

Jeremiah grabbed his phone to search for his next book. He got distracted by a notification on LinkedIn and found himself scrolling through the newsfeed. He happened upon a post from a friend he met in one of his self-help book groups. The post caught Jeremiah's attention and dialogue in the comments ensued:

—

Ajala Pilgrim • 1st
Co-Founder at Annex Group
4mo • Edited • 🌐

Self Help Books.... Genuine or Fraud?

I have had a lot of discussion with friends who believe these books are pointless. They've tried reading but nothing ever changes.
And for some people these books are something that only 'wantapreneurs' read — books that trick people into wishing their way to success while sitting on the couch.

I think your approach to these books are very important. One of my favourite and the books that I swear by is the 7 habits of highly successful people. Ive read it about 10 times and I take notes and try to form these habits that I think apply to me.

These books however are no blueprint to success, reading it once wont make you successful. It's important to practice what you read.
The truth is most of these books are telling us things we already know. What is important is applying it in a context that makes sense to you, your life and career.

A perfect example is the "wake up early" to be more efficient.

While that may have applied to many for me it didn't. I work better at night and quite often I go to bed when most persons are now waking up. Nobody defines when my day starts and ends, we all have the same 24 hours.

All this to say Application and Context is important.

Self Help Books? I say Genuine

What about you?

#motivation #selfhelp

Jeremiah

This post spoke to me man. I say genuine also! I just finished *The 7 Habits of Highly Successful People* coincidentally. I learned so much!

Ajala

Glad to hear it. What piece of information jumped out to you the most how will you apply it in your life?

Jeremiah paused to think about what he learned while reading the book. He grew more and more embarrassed as time elapsed. He was embarrassed because he could not pull one useful piece of information from his memory. "This is really peculiar. I just finished this book. . . . Why is it that I can't recall any information from it?" he wondered. He began thinking about the other nine books that he read prior and had similar difficulties in recalling what he had learned.

He signed off of LinkedIn and began rummaging through his room in search of his notebook. Luckily, he took notes while he read. He finally found it and quickly opened it to the first page. There it was in big bold writing: Goal: Read 50+ books in one year. Reading his goal brought an immediate smile to Jeremiah's face. His cheerful expression quickly disappeared, unfortunately. As he flipped through the pages he realized how scattered all the notes were. He could not tell what piece of information came from what book. It was a sloppy mess.

Upon further inspection, he noticed a note that was not only written in all capital letters but underlined with arrows pointing towards it. The note read: **IMMEDIATELY INCORPORATE THE USEFUL**

—

INFORMATION YOU LEARN INTO YOUR DAILY LIFE. What was glaringly obvious to Jeremiah's girlfriend was now apparent to him. In his journey to get to his reading goal, he had forgotten the most important thing: to learn! Jeremiah was disappointed in himself but determined to fix his mistake.

He tried his best to create some order to the notes he had scribbled in his notebook. The most useful advice was transferred to sticky notes and stuck up on his wall. He also made a mental note to re-read the ten books he had previously finished. On a piece of paper, he wrote down the following question, "What have you learned today?" He stuck this in his reading area as a gentle reminder to focus when he is reading and not to read for reading's sake. His girlfriend stepped in the room and slyly said, "Well, look at you finally making some changes." Jeremiah laughed embarrassingly upon hearing her words.

Jeremiah returned to Ajala's post and commented the following:

Jeremiah
Hey, thanks so much for posting this. I realized I was so focused on hitting a reading target that I wasn't retaining the information. I needed to see this so I could shift my mindset.

***

Strive to be a life-long learner. In this respect, don't get so caught up in the numbers game. For example, if you have a target number of books to read, focus more on learning and retaining what you learn than hitting the targeted amount. The more you learn and apply, the more

—

valuable you become to yourself and others. Note the importance of not only learning but applying what you learn. Boasting that you've read a certain book or finished a set number of books, it's all useless if you do not process what you learn and integrate that knowledge into your life. When you can do this habitually, each book or new piece of information can become a potential new skill waiting to be unlocked.

A Parent's Promise

Affirmation: I pave the way for the future.

Veronica looked down at her sleeping newborn in her eggshell white crib. "Such a precious sight," she thought to herself. She could not believe what a perfect little thing she had created. She marveled at her daughter for quite some time that afternoon. She kissed her sleeping baby and quietly slipped away, closing the door ever so quietly.

She joined her mother in the living room. As they sat and chatted over some tea, Veronica began telling her mother about all the things she wanted to provide for her baby that weren't available to her. Her mom grew quiet and Veronica immediately apologized because she realized that her comments may have come across as a bit insensitive. Her mother grew up poor and lived in a modest home. There were many things that Veronica asked for when she was an adolescent that her parents simply weren't able to provide.

Her mother was a housekeeper and her dad picked up odd jobs around the neighborhood to provide for the family. Veronica's mother broke the silence with a hearty smile absolving her daughter of any guilt. She was smiling because she knew her daughter meant no offense by the statement. Her mother felt proud of how her daughter climbed out of poverty. She took solace in knowing that although they were poor, they made sure to provide for their children.

Veronica's mom got up and walked over to a picture of Veronica on her graduation day. Her mother, who was unable to receive a formal education, made a promise to herself that when she had children, they would have access to a proper education. Veronica smiled because her mother's promise was actualized. Not only did she have a master's degree in finance, but her younger sister Rayanna was an engineer.

Veronica thought about what she was able to accomplish because of her parents' sacrifice. The extra shifts they picked up to pay for their children's way through grad school. The funds they pooled to help them purchase their first car. Their dad drove them anywhere they needed to go. When her sister was in the library late at night studying, her father would always be the one to get up at whatever hour—1 am, 2 am, it did not matter—to retrieve her. It was the same when her sister had late shifts at work.

Veronica recognized that she would not be half the person she was without her parents' sacrifice. She remembered that when the coursework was becoming impossible and the anxiety had become stifling, her mother was always there to keep her motivated. Veronica recalled how proud she felt when she was finally able to chip in more at home. Equipped with a master's degree, she was eventually able to get a high-paying job to not only start building her own life but assisting her parents with the bills.

Walking down memory lane with her mother, Veronica accidentally bumped a book off the countertop table. Cries from the other room could be heard echoing from the next room. She picked up her crying daughter and began comforting her in her arms. At that moment, Veronica began, again, to think about all of the things she would provide for her daughter. She was committed to making the kind of sacrifices for her daughter that her parents made for her.

***

Our parents want the best for us. The sacrifices they make for us help to expand our opportunity for a successful life. Take some time to reflect on all your parents have provided for you. If you're not aware of what sacrifices were made, it can be worthwhile to find out. You may be surprised to learn what they went through. Through learning about their experiences, you will see how deep their love runs. Cherish the time you have with your parents and take all the good they put into you and pass it onto your children.

Buff Body Loading

Affirmation: I nourish my body with healthy food and exercise.

Dion woke up reluctantly, as he did every morning. He hoped this morning he would be different. That he would shift his gaze downwards and see a miracle: a flat stomach with "cheesegrater-esque" abs—like the type you see in those magazines. Every morning he would somehow hope that his body would revert to its younger days, his college days when he was super active. Those days were filled with gym, sports, and crunches. His diet was salads and cheap rum.

Dion thought about how subtly it all happened. He left college and got a job. He continued to frequent the gym but each week he would work out less and less. His day job was monotonous and Dion started to snack to fill the dead space with something. For Dion, that something was chocolate! He became oddly obsessed with the stuff. He would stock up at the beginning of each month and leave mountains of chocolate bars in his desk drawer.

He glanced at his rounded stomach and caressed it. The fat seemed to form a hermetic seal around his midsection. His own body sickened him. His friends were fed up with his constant complaining because according to them, "You aren't even fat." "What do they know," he thought. "All I can see are the days where I was in perfect condition. I can't help but compare myself to that person. Sure, the circumstances and environment were different, but I can achieve that now. It's not too late," he kept reassuring himself.

As Dion finally made his way to the bathroom and began brushing his teeth, he began to plot how often he would have to work out and what he'd have to eat to transform his body over the next three months. This was the fifth time over two months that he considered a plan like this. "I will eat only salads and bake chicken, run each morning before work and lift in the evening after work," he schemed. The plan was perfect. He would look like the trainer in his gym.

Day 1 of "Buff Body Loading" as he named it and he surprised himself by waking up before his 4 am alarm. Overly excited before he went to bed, he was already sleeping in his running clothes. That way he could be out the door without a fuss. The goal was to complete a hot and sweaty four-mile run. The last time he ran four miles straight was about seven months ago. But he figured a savage jolt to the body would help ignite his latent fitness spirit. Two miles in and he was about to vomit.

He resigned himself to a half attempt and jumped off the treadmill. "A job decently done," he thought proudly. "I owe myself a hearty breakfast after that," he thought. He made an egg-white veggie omelet with turkey bacon on the side and black coffee with no sugar. His body felt nourished and he felt empowered.

He wrapped up a day of work. All day, he felt like a horse that plowed the soil. The morning run did not help his energy levels. Yet gym time had come. He rushed over to the gym and put in a solid two-hour workout. Afterward, he was completely exhausted, so he decided on an early night and mentally prepared himself to go through the torture all over again.

Day two, three, and four all went on as planned, although Dion could not help himself and ate a few chocolate bars each day. He needed to find sweet relief and to keep his energy up somehow, he rationalized. "Man does not live on salad alone," he reasoned.

He took a break on the weekend and squinted his eyes as he looked in the mirror to see what little physical results he made (there were none). He had a relaxing weekend grimacing at the thought of the coming torture of Monday morning. That morning, he got up early to run. He thought recovery meant that he would feel, you know, recovered but his body felt more drained even though he took a break on the weekend. When he was younger he bounced back in an instant. He held that thought and used it to power through.

He rose bright and early Monday morning. It was 4:30 am and he was a bit late but, "No big deal," he thought. Instead of jumping out of bed instantly, he convinced himself that it would be a good idea to check all his social media platforms to see what he missed last night as he went to bed early. What felt like ten minutes turned into an hour and soon enough, it was too late to run. He was both angry at himself for getting distracted and all too happy to have missed that run.

After work, Dion thought to himself, "I already missed running this morning, what would be the big deal if I miss gym today. I will start fresh tomorrow for sure." To no surprise a week passed and his running shoes nor the gym had seen him since the week before. The next Monday, he woke up and glanced at his stomach. A wave of disgust flooded his body. He had gone full circle.

"This time needs to be different," he thought. He decided not to sell himself any dreams. He got up and looked at himself in the mirror. He then said aloud, "I acknowledged what I looked like in the past and I accept that it's in the past. The futile internal fight I keep having is doing me no good. This is who I am and I'm okay with it." He tried to let go of that past version of himself so he could see all the positive features of his current self.

He made a goal for how he would exercise and eat moving forward. This time, though, he started very small. He acknowledged that for the person he was and the life he lived, it was less important for him to be the buff college student he was back in the day. It was enough to run or go to the gym twice or three times during the week. It was enough for him to eat his junk food but in moderation. He was okay with achieving what he believed was within his physical means and of course, he could strive for more once he was consistent.

***

Sometimes we can find ourselves anchored to the past. We compare ourselves to what we were which can become a torturous experience. As your circumstances, needs, and wants change, allow your perception of yourself to change as well. Often that change in perception will produce a shift in the goals you set and the results you expect. But first, be honest with yourself and take note of what's important to you.

Autopilot Malfunction

Affirmation: I prioritize what's most important to me on a daily basis.

Nichelle twiddled her thumbs nervously. She had not made eye contact yet. Her gaze was fixed on her fingers. This was the first time she had made an appointment with a life coach. She had never felt the need before. However, by what felt like divine intervention, she kept seeing this particular coach's motivational videos on LinkedIn. His most recent video captioned "Autopilot Malfunction" hit the nail on the head for her. In the video, he spoke about going with the flow and how it can lead to an unsatisfied life. The video shined the brightest light imaginable on a challenge she was facing. Nichelle thought, "What do I have to lose? Let's give it a go."

On their first meeting, the following conversation ensued:

Coach: "So Nichelle, from your earlier message you said that you weren't happy with how your life is going right now. Could you give me some details on what makes you feel this way?"

Nichelle: "Well . . . for the past couple of weeks I feel like all I do is work. I have not been feeling very fulfilled and I desperately want to spend more time with my daughter. She's four."

Coach: "Okay, I see. What is it that you do for a living?"

Nichelle: "I work as an HR professional."

Coach: "What did you do before this?"

Nichelle: "I was doing graphic design. The switch to HR was pretty random. The company I was doing graphic work for found that I was very organized. They had a position open up in HR and the supervisor, I guess, took a liking to me and kept pushing me to apply. She said she would give me a recommendation. I figured why not. It would be something new and the pay was better than what I was currently getting. I got the job and although the work was not what I was accustomed to, the experiences were new and refreshing every day. It felt like I had found a new calling. I love graphic design but I grew to love the HR work as well."

Coach: "Hmmm . . . I see. What changed about the work exactly?

Nichelle: "After about a year I was promoted to a higher position which I was excited about. As expected, it required more work but I was excited about the new challenge. The work, however, became overwhelming. I found that I had less and less time to do the things I loved to do."

Coach: "Like what?"

Nichelle: "I got into graphic design because I love to create. I used to draft a new doodle every single day and post it up on social media. It was a kinda ritual for me. A way to practice my creative expression. I also love to write short stories. I don't even think about what I will write. I simply sit down and the words come to me, you know? I also love spending time with my daughter. She is the light of my world, my whole heartbeat, and every minute I get to spend with her is everything."

Coach: "So I want you to do a simple exercise for me. Close your eyes and clear your mind. Now I want you to outline what a perfect day would look like for you."

Nichelle: "Hmmm . . . well . . . assuming it's a workday and not a weekend, I would get up and do some morning yoga. Then take a shower and cuddle with my daughter for a bit. Then get her up and prepare breakfast for the both of us after I got her ready for daycare. After I dropped her off at daycare, I would go to this park I like and spend about a couple of minutes enjoying the atmosphere and creating a doodle on my tablet. I'd then go to work and after work was over I'd write a short story or two then spend the rest of the day with my daughter."

Coach: "Sounds like a great day. In comparison what is your typical day like now?"

Nichelle: "Um . . . I typically wake up late because I work late the night before. My mom has been helping me with my daughter so she gets her ready and drops her off at daycare while I hustle to get ready for work. Once I get to work, I'm there until late, and rinse and repeat for the next day."

Coach: "Well the problem should be pretty clear now. There is a big disparity between the life you want to live and the life you are currently living. You stopped doing many things that you loved to do. You got sucked into work so deeply that you don't make time for anything else. Sometimes opportunities are dropped into our lap and we see them as a sign to act. As was the case with you discovering your new interest in HR. But when you allow yourself to go with the flow too often or operate on autopilot, as I call it, your actions tend to be reactive as opposed to proactive. It's clear you love the challenge of the HR job but you need to strike a balance between work and the things you love to do, or you will continue to be unhappy and unsatisfied."

Nichelle fell deathly silent as she processed the information. What he was saying was true and as clear as day to her. How could she have not seen it? She was so caught up in life that she did not realize that she was no longer in control. The coach outlined a few daily activities that

—

Nichelle could do to better her days. These included finding a morning routine and resuming her daily doodles and story writing. He also told her to outline time blocks during the day for spending quality time with her daughter. Nichelle took the advice and began incorporating it into her day-to-day schedule. She remained overwhelmed with work for a bit but prioritizing her needs again made life feel much more balanced.

***

It's easy to just go with the flow in life. But going with the flow can lead to unhappiness and a feeling of loss. Take note of what you love to do and what you want to prioritize in your life. Be intentional with your planning and actions. Avoid investing too much of your time into activities that don't bring you joy. Create the life you want to live by being proactive about your planning and decision-making.

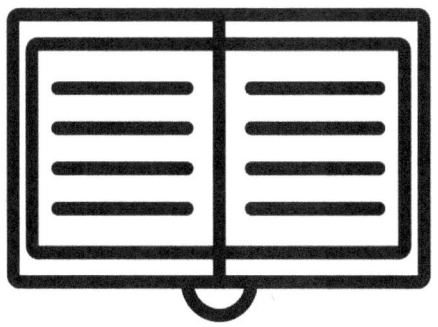

The Millennial Mind

Affirmation: Fear does not control me. I create my own destiny.

There are few times in your life where the chips line up perfectly. The experience I had, however, made me think otherwise. It all started in September 2019 when I had a great idea. I had been a personal development coach for about two years. Each week I saw a host of clients and helped them better their lives. I focused on everything that pertained to achieving success and finding purpose.

I had completed work with a client whose life had significantly changed for the better. The work I was doing was having a positive impact but there are only so many clients I could see daily. Then an idea burst into my mind as though it was always right there in front of me. "How can

I help more people without physically being present?" Write a book! It was such a no-brainer moment.

Now, equipped only with an idea, I decided to do the Millennial thing and I went straight to social media to seek positive confirmation of my idea from my community. I put out a poll asking my Instagram followers about what they felt would be the better title, "The Millennial Mind" or "Adulting 101." The results were overwhelmingly in favor of the former. Not only that but I got a multitude of direct messages in my inbox from people who were excited about the book and encouraging me to write it.

That was all the validation I needed to start writing. The only problem was I knew nothing about writing a book nor did I know the process of publishing, distributing, or even marketing a book. As quickly as those roadblocks entered my mind so did the fear. The fear spread quickly within me like a poisonous gas being pumped into a sealed room. It was all so suffocating.

To quell some of my fears, I Googled every last question I had about the writing and publishing process:

Q How do I write a good book?	×	🎤

Q How do I self-publish?	×	🎤

Q How the hell do I put a book on Amazon?	×	🎤

Q How to market a book?	×	🎤

Q Self-publishing versus publishing companies?	×	🎤

This frantic search led me to many videos, podcasts, books, and profiles of bestselling authors. I knew that I needed to spend a significant amount of time on learning because, in my current state, I was ill-equipped for the task ahead of me. After one month of intense focus, I was able to read four books, watch at least twenty videos, and finished two online courses. Not only that, but I also direct messaged multiple bestselling authors asking them for advice. Of the 200 or so messages sent, I was lucky enough to receive five replies. The advice I got from those who replied made it worth it. The summary of the advice I received was to think about what my market needs, write with a goal in mind, focus on my niche, and treat the entire process as a business.

I was now ready to begin writing. Interestingly enough, the best advice I got on the writing process came from my younger sister. She wrote a fiction book a while back and she said to write every single day. So that's what I did. Each morning for two months I wrote and wrote and wrote. I even wrote when I didn't feel like doing so. I wrote when the words made little sense and when they strung together perfectly. It was after those two months that I realized how much work it was to write a book.

I finished the manuscript and soon after, I began the publishing process. I decided to go the route of self-publishing because I had full confidence that I could create and execute a stellar plan. I followed the advice and knowledge I amassed over the prior months and formed a strategy. I then brought a team together to help make the plan work. An editor, marketing expert, PR expert, graphic artist, and assistant. We all pitched in to make the plan whole and went to work.

The venture was going to cost me a dizzying amount of money, so I decided to take out a loan to pay for everything. "Why not commit wholly," I reasoned. I figured I could at least sell enough books monthly to repay my loan. It was a risk, a calculated risk that I was comfortable with, or so I thought. It was only when I signed on the dotted lines and the money was transferred to my account did the true weight of it all hit me. This was happening. There was no going back. I have to perform or die. That may be a little overdramatic but that's how I was feeling. I once again felt the toxic gas of fear occupying space in my mind. Unfortunately, this time the fumes were thicker, and gaining more knowledge was not going to air out the room. The only thing that would inhibit my anxiety was a massive amount of sustained action.

I worked and worked and worked! Putting my all into the plan. Days turned to weeks. Weeks turned into months and it was soon time for my book to launch. Leading up to the book's release, most things were going smoothly. My team was doing their part. The only hiccups were late work being submitted from time to time. "No big disaster there," I thought to myself as I mentally and physically began relaxing my tense, overworked body. I probably should have knocked on wood at that moment because things were about to get immensely difficult.

All the news outlets worldwide were overburdened with covering Covid-19 and to my dismay, my little island of Trinidad and Tobago began receiving its first imported cases. The government reacted quickly and immediately shut down the country in hopes of quelling any potential spread. This shutdown coincided with the launch of my book which I'd worked on tirelessly over the past five months. I was completely and utterly crushed. I was not only suffocating in fear but drowning in it. The fear did not take the form of gas this time around but a liquid. It encapsulated my entire mind. I could not tell up from down and I felt powerless to do anything.

I was a month away from launching my book and for two weeks I did absolutely nothing. Crippled by fear, I could not lift a finger. I just sulked in my room watching Netflix for hours on end hoping that the problem would solve itself. I checked updates from the people I hired but did not reply to any messages, that was until I received an email from my editor requesting that I confirm some changes that he made to a chapter in my book. This change was very time sensitive so I had no choice but to get it done sooner rather than later.

I began reading the chapter of my book that needed attention and I could not stop myself from laughing. I had read the following sequence of words that I wrote . . . which were ironic.

"We all have our different struggles and we all suffer at some point to overcome them or blissfully ignore them by cleverly rationalizing that we are fine and things will get better (they won't get better if you do nothing by the way).

We don't realize, though, that life is all grey. We are constantly in a state of figuring things out and there is always something new to overcome.

Empowerment comes from the acceptance that this is your life. It may not be perfect but it belongs to you. It may not be exactly the way you want it to be but that's okay. No one's life is exactly the way they want it to be and no one is without some level of worry or stress. Even when you achieve the things you want, some new to worry about will appear and prod you to work towards overcoming it."

It was as though I was transmitting advice to myself from the past. How could I have been such a hypocrite? The words I wrote spoke to exactly what I was experiencing yet I was giving up!? "This is not the end," I exclaimed. I literally and figuratively dusted myself off (there were snack crumbs everywhere) and got myself together.

I started by calling up everyone on the team and began brainstorming new ideas for the book launch event. Together we came up with a virtual book launch concept that was just crazy enough to work. Two weeks later with an inconceivable amount of work and planning, the virtual launch date finally arrived. With the use of a studio, I streamed live from Instagram and wowed the viewers with all the frills and thrills of a book launch experience they could never have expected. There were performances, a host, giveaways, and speeches. It was truly amazing. What was noteworthy was that in a time where Instagram live events were saturating the platform because everyone was stuck at home and starved for entertainment, with my meager 3,000 followers, I was able to pull 2,500 viewers that evening.

The hard work, risk, and planning paid off. The launch was a success and helped to propel the sales of my book to numbers that continue to amaze me. As of writing this, I have sold my 1,000th book, just six months after my book launch. And it still feels like the sky's the limit.

***

Fear can have such great power over us. It creates invisible chains that bind our arms and feet and stunt our actions and potential greatness. When we overcome our fears and break free from those chains, we now open the doors to vast opportunities. Without fear we can venture into new territories and gift ourselves the chance of doing something extraordinary.

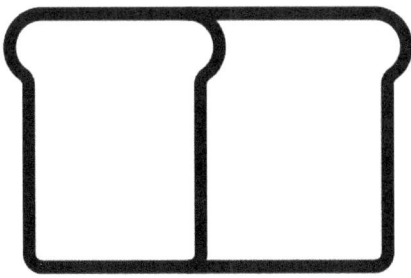

Krumbled Dreams

Affirmation: I renew my goals and dreams.

Devon had a set vision for his life. He knew exactly how he wanted it to play out. His vision was laser-focused ever since he was a young boy. He knew he wanted to have his fun in his teenage years, find "the girl" in his twenties, marry "the girl" in his mid-twenties, have 2.5 children before he got to his early thirties. And he wanted to build on top of it all so he could provide for his family.

He even had a deep understanding of why he wanted his life to play out in this order. He recalled how his father left him and his mother to fend for themselves. He felt a deep hurt for not being good enough to keep his father around. He felt forced to be the man of the house at an early age and that became a major piece of his identity over time.

Devon's vision for his life was playing out just as he imagined. He partied from his late teens into his early twenties. He enjoyed all the thrills that someone with a car and money could have. Girls, alcohol, and parties were his weekly diet until he could do it no more. Once he got a foot in the door of his twenties he began to pivot. He was on the hunt for a stable lasting relationship. There were two or three women that came close to fitting the bill, but one woman finally embodied his idea of "the girl." She was everything he wanted and more. Her name was Saran and she made him want to be better. She challenged all the parts of him that needed improvement and they helped each other become better all whilst creating a beautiful life around each other. It seemed as if Saran would surely be his wife.

Five years later and a walk down the aisle and Devon was happily married. He and Saran eventually had two kids, a girl and a boy. The family had a home, two vehicles, and lived in a quiet and safe neighborhood. Saran worked as a sales agent and Devon ran Krumbs, their home-based bakery. With the skills he acquired from previously working at a bakery and Saran's hard work, Krumbs was flourishing. Life for Devon was playing out perfectly.

Day in and day out, it was business as usual. He and Saran tended to their kids, he baked, made deliveries, and developed the business. Devon stayed busy and soon began to develop a consistent chest pain. It did not make any sense. He went to several doctors, racking up quite a hefty bill in the process, but they all said the same thing, that there was nothing physically wrong with him.

After a while, he found it more and more difficult to sleep at night. His mind would stay active and he could not, for the life of him, find relief. This proved problematic because when the day began and he had to deal with kids, baking, and deliveries, it made a typically long day feel even longer. The lack of sleep also seemed to trigger more chest pain. He felt like he could not take any more of it and was willing to try anything.

Saran suggested that he see a personal development coach. Devon rolled his eyes at the idea of seeing someone who was going to lecture him on his feelings and all that nonsense. At this point, however, he did not have many options, so he decided to try it out. A week later, Devon reluctantly sat down with the coach to get to the root of the problem. For the first thirty minutes the coach would ask Devon questions about his life. The coach asked about his typical day, his diet, how he started his mornings, and how he ended his days. He asked Devon about the plans he had for himself and his family. He also asked how he was planning to take action on all his plans now and in the future.

Devon answered all the questions, although he had quickly become impatient. "What does any of this have to do with my sleeping problem and chest pain," he thought to himself angrily. The coach paused for a long while as he jotted down notes in his tiny notebook. He then looked Devon directly in his eye, and for the first time during their session, started speaking sentences that weren't questions. He said the following:

"Devon, I must commend you on the life that you have built for yourself. It is admirable that you had a vision for how you wanted your life to turn out and then you went for it with full commitment and conviction. You achieved everything you set out to achieve and there was no doubt in your mind that you would do so. If everyone had the drive and confidence that you have, we would be a remarkable country. That being said, based on what you have told me there are only two issues I see that are holding you back right now. 1) You stopped dreaming and 2) Your internalized persona of being "the man of the house" has taken on a toxic form within you."

Devon was baffled by this breakdown. "What hot garbage," he thought to himself. The coach continued, "I can tell by your facial expression that you think I am talking nonsense but let me break it down. You were heavily driven by your vision. Marriage, kids, a house, and enough money to keep it all going. You have reached those goals but the question is, now what? You have not thought past this point. You have attained what you obsessively labored over for most of your life but the crucial mistake you made was not updating your dreams or goals. What will Devon work towards from this point? What is most important to his future and the future of his family? Is your new vision to franchise your bakery and take it all over the nation? What is the vision you have for your children's education? What about the continued love and happiness of you and your wife? You now have the great opportunity to dream again and create a new vision moving forward. Just like your old vision, a new vision will give you renewed purpose and drive."

Devon remained quiet to allow the coach's words to settle in his mind. "Had I stopped aiming for anything?" he questioned. He could not think of anything he was aiming for outside of survival. He was in default mode. The coach went on, "When you allow yourself to dream again and set goals for the future, you will find that you are more focused and better able to prioritize your days, weeks, and months. Now, to the second problem. Because you have been the "man of the house" for the majority of your life, you don't know any other way. In your current life, you have taken it to an extreme. You take on the heavy responsibility of providing for your family solely upon your shoulders. You do this to the detriment of your health. All that worrying, stress, and anxiety has reached a tipping point. This is why you struggle to relax and rest. You can't flip the off switch because you are always on and activated. This explains the pain in your chest. Learn to rely on your wife more because she is there to help. That being said, you need to create "Devon time" every day. Find moments to do the things you love, the things that help you relax. Resting does not mean you are wasting time. It is part of being a healthy and functional human being. As it stands right now, you don't do anything for Devon. You work and you take care of your family."

It was all becoming clear to Devon. All this time he thought he was being the person he needed to be. What he was actually doing was taking on too much. He acknowledged what the coach was saying and they worked out a plan on what he would do moving forward. Saran would take some of the responsibilities of the business off of her husband. Something she had been trying to do for years. They made a list of activities that Devon would do just for him. He joined a run group and began jogging every other day and even picked up golf. Devon made a written list of the new goals for himself, his kids, and their business. He found that this made it easy to prioritize actions and to know what was important. It was as if Devon was back to dreaming again.

Three weeks into Devon's new lifestyle, his lack of sleep and chest pains were a thing of the past. He found that he had more energy and drive daily. And he looked forward to his "Devon time." He was excited about his new outlook on life and confident that his actions were leading him where he wanted to go.

***

You can put your all into something for so long that when you achieve it, you never ask yourself, "What's next?" If you have accomplished your dreams, remember that there is still life to be lived and your dreams may need updating. When you don't ask yourself "what's next?" you can easily fall into a trap of complacency. Dreams allow you the opportunity to peer into a world where you have everything you ever desired. Move your dreams into goals and you are one step closer to a new beginning.

Trauma Overruled

Affirmation: I overcome every obstacle that gets in the way of my success.

Trigger Warning: This story contains triggering content on sexual abuse.

Amy sat on a park bench, lost in thought for what seemed like an eternity. Today was a special day but her thoughts were heavily locked in the past. Just then a gentle breeze blew and she remembered the cool wind that would make its way into her room on occasion. She always wondered how the wind made it from the open door, through the living room then to her room.

An older gentleman walked by snapping Amy out of the memory. She gripped her shirt tightly as he passed and was pulled into another memory, one she always tried to avoid. It was painful. She recalled when she was around thirteen years old and her body began to develop and how much joy this brought her. She liked the way she was growing physically. Around the same time, her uncle would visit more and more frequently. He was not a blood relative but he was in her life for so long that he was treated like family. She remembered not thinking much of it back then because why would she.

The incident happened one day when her mom was at work and she was home babysitting her siblings. Her uncle showed up unexpectedly. This was strange but nothing to cause concern. Amy remembered him reasoning with her to join him in the car because he had something to show her. She felt strange about the request and refused. This angered him and a struggle ensued. The details always get pretty hazy about what happened during the altercation but luckily her mother arrived home and was furious with her uncle. They shouted at each other for what felt like forever and he eventually left.

Amy reached into her handbag to grab a napkin to dry the tears flowing from her eyes. That memory was always difficult to think about. She soon regained her composure and allowed the heavy energy to pass. She then smiled as she thought about her aunt. Her aunt was not a blood relative either but a close family friend who visited frequently. She thought about how much she looked up to her aunt who was a big shot lawyer. When Amy was younger her aunt visited one day and noticed that she had not been herself ever since that visit from her uncle. But

Amy tried to act normally and take care of her siblings as her mom had picked up another job. She just didn't want to be a bother.

Her aunt had begun questioning her about her change in mood and her silence. Amy did not remember exactly what she told her aunt but she does remember vividly what happened after that conversation. Her aunt spoke with her mom and Amy never saw the uncle again. As Amy got older, she began putting the pieces together on what occurred with her uncle. Amy realized that her aunt saved her from a bad situation that could have been made worse. Her adoration of her aunt grew exponentially ever since that realization. But not only that, her sudden interest in becoming a lawyer, just like her aunt, also grew. Amy began to dream again. She spoke to her aunt about it many times and her aunt helped in any way that she could.

Amy eventually decided to go to law school. Whenever Amy needed textbooks or money for school fees, her aunt was there to chip in. Her aunt even passed along old exam papers and notes as Amy graduated to higher and higher levels. Amy's drive for success was dissolving the constraints around her. Amy chuckled as she remembered how many late nights of studying it took for her to get to this point. Law school was still the hardest thing she ever had to do. She never knew she had so much strength within her. She wanted to see her circumstances change, not only for herself but for her siblings.

Amy then snapped out of her thoughts as her aunt and her mom were calling for her. Their smiling faces filled her with so much joy. She ran over to them and hugged them both. She then walked over to her classmates to take a picture on the steps of the court as any new attorney starting their journey would do.

***

You may believe that you can easily sweep painful memories under the rug and live your life. However, those memories will eventually manifest themselves in some way in your life. Most of the time that manifestation is something negative. Facing the pain of a bad memory can be terrifying. It can be earth-shattering. But facing it can also be the beginning of healing. If you're holding on to a painful memory, think of the person you could be if you allowed yourself to heal. That healing can open the door to more of your potential which may take you to unimaginable heights.

Supporting Resource

National Domestic Violence Hotline 1 (868) 800 SAVE (7283)

DEAD MONEY!

Affirmation: Even with life's challenges I welcome growth.

Michelle stormed out of the room and slammed her bedroom door behind her. Her frustration had reached its peak. She was fuming, tired of the constant arguments with her parents. As soon as she turned twenty-six, it was as if a switch was flipped within her parents. Now every little thing she did would rile them up. She felt like they could no longer live together.

In the latest episode of "Get on Michelle's Nerves," her mother took the dishes out of the sink and placed them on her bed. She claimed it was Michelle's day to wash and had neglected her responsibilities. But Michelle thought that she gave her mother a heads up that she would be working late so she would not be able to do the dishes on time. Her mother had no recollection of that conversation. Suffice it to say, Michelle was getting completely and utterly fed up with the arrangement.

In the Caribbean it is an accepted norm that children live with their parents well into adulthood, even past the age of thirty. This is especially so given the state of the economy where paying for rent is more difficult. Michelle thought about moving out numerous times, but two words would always come to mind that stopped her dead in her tracks: DEAD MONEY! She was very frugal and she had good reason to be. She had grand plans for her future which would require a lot of money. She wanted to get a Ph.D., buy a car and purchase her own home. It was manageable paying for insurance, daily expenses, attempting to save, and paying a "contribution" to the household. But her parents demanded a greater contribution month after month, and on top of that, the daily hostile energy they gave off towards her was wearing her down. It was beginning to appear as though moving out was more and more a viable option.

Michelle sat and thought about her predicament for a long time. In her internal monologue, her decision came down to mental health versus financial growth. Her relationship with her parents was deteriorating by the day but at least she could save the majority of her income after expenses. On the other hand, she could not stand to hear her parents' voices anymore. Her agitation at the situation was also beginning to affect her relationships with her friends and boyfriend because she was always on edge or complaining about her situation at home.

She took the next two weeks to deliberate on a decision. Whatever she decided could not be taken lightly. In those two weeks, she spoke to friends who were renting. She found the feedback pretty interesting. More than a few of her friends talked about loving the freedom and that the new responsibilities of being independent made them more financially responsible. "Maybe it was one of those things you had to experience to understand," she thought.

At the end of the two weeks, Michelle came to a decision. It was time to move out! She broke the news to her parents and typical of Caribbean parents, they were sad that their baby was leaving them. Michelle, though excited for the next stage, was notably fearful of the unknown. She wondered what would happen if she lost her job or forgot to turn off the stove and burn down the building. She allowed herself to go through the motions and eventually settled down.

After moving in all her stuff and getting settled, Michelle reveled in her new space. Her roommate was a good friend of hers. She felt so much relief for not having to deal with her parents anymore and a giant weight was lifted off her shoulders. Today was the first day of the rest of her life. She was excited.

Then like an avalanche rolling to the base of a mountain, the dream came tumbling down. Reality smacked Michelle on day one! Typically, her dad would be up at 6 am for his early morning run and the noise he made would always wake Michelle up, annoying her to no end. However, the noise would get her up in time to get ready for work whereas she never needed to set an alarm. Now on her own, with no alarm set, she woke up late. Worse yet, she had no breakfast or lunch because her mom was not there as usual to prep food for the week.

Michelle rushed to work and had to deal with the slight humiliation of arriving to work late. She was a bit annoyed that she had to buy breakfast and lunch. Her annoyance soon turned to worry as she was spending money that was meant to be saved. After a long day, she slumped into bed. Curled up next to her were her regrets for leaving home. Things were different and she began doubting herself. "Living on your own is a responsibility," she thought but she was determined to make it work.

The next day she dragged herself out of bed and prepped lunch for the rest of the week. She even made breakfast for the next day and popped it in the fridge. Her roommate even joined in and gave her a variety of delicious and cheap recipes that she could use. Her roommate was a real pro at this it seemed. It was weirdly exciting for Michelle as she never thought that she would be pumped to prep meals. "Adulting for you," she thought. Over the next few days, she enlisted the help of a financial advisor. She wanted to take her finances to the next level. She had to make up for the new exorbitant monthly expense that was rent. After an hour-long session, she realized how much of her decisions and goals were just "winging it." Now, she felt more comfortable with what percentage of her money would go into savings and investments. She even chuckled at the fact that she finally understood what "diversified portfolio" meant.

After her first month, once the rent money left her account, Michelle came to a realization. She needed to make more money! She pulled out her trusty portable whiteboard and began listing all the activities that could potentially bring in more income. Her top two choices were a better-paid position at work and copywriting jobs as a side hustle. There was a time while in college when she did copywriting work for a company. She made enough money to fund her party-goer lifestyle, so she figured why not reignite that relationship.

The next day she was a woman on a mission. She spoke to her manager about available positions and applied to the two that seemed more feasible for her to get. She also emailed the company that she did the copywriting work for to see if they have any work for her. After some interviews and waiting a week, Michelle was bummed to learn that she did not get any of the two jobs she applied for at her current employer. But on the bright side, she got useful feedback from her boss on managerial courses she could take to make her more likely to get a higher position when one became available. Her manager also promised to give her a shining recommendation once she had done the courses.

Some good news came when the company she did copywriting work for in college eventually got back to her. They were doing a major overhaul for a financial company's website and they needed help to re-do blogs and general information on the site. They wanted to enlist her for the project. The pay was not grand, but it was additional income!

Michelle woke up one Saturday to see a message from her mom inviting her over for lunch. She had not seen her parents in many weeks and she felt excited to update them on everything that was going on. She arrived for lunch and visiting her parents was like nothing she had experienced before. They were chatting as though they were old friends. She felt compelled to share with them in ways she would not have when she lived with them. Typically, she'd answer with "I'm fine" or "Things are going okay" but she found herself giving the play-by-play with all her exciting new experiences. The best part was they sent her off with bags full of groceries which mean that she would definitely be visiting often.

***

Moving on to the next stage in your life can be intimidating. You won't always know what will occur. Often, a new chapter of life will bring on experiences and growth that you could not imagine. Sometimes you just need to make the dive and learn from the splash. While the outcome is impossible to know, when taking a risk like moving out on your own, weigh the pros and cons and seek advice from those who have done it successfully.

Self-Prescribed

Affirmation: I make time for self-care.

Bright-eyed and inquisitive describes the beginning of most student's academic journeys. With the vision of saving lives on his mind, Alex was proud to call himself a doctor. In his mind anyway, as he was still a medical student. But a boy can dream, no? The allure of saving lives quickly disappeared when the work began. Class after class leading into exam after exam. Each week passed with increasing intensity and it was only year one!

Yet nothing would put a wrench in Alex's enthusiasm. This profession was his calling. It ran in his blood and DNA. His great grandfather, grandfather, father, and brother were all doctors. It was predestined. Alex recalled receiving a toy stethoscope as a gift when he was a young boy. Medicine was serious business for his family. Failure was never an option.

Six long grueling years later and he was finally done with medical school. Some days it felt like he was going to throw his laptop in the trash, throw his hands over his head, and give up. But he persevered. He let out the biggest sigh of relief and for the first time in years, he fully relaxed, if only for a week or two.

Alex was well aware that medical school was just the warm-up. He still had residency to weather and working as a doctor was no cakewalk either, but he was up to the challenge. If medical school was walking a tightrope with a balancing beam, residency was walking the same tight rope with the balancing beam, while two heavy bricks were placed in on both shoulders. "This was what I prepared for," he told himself.

The experience was grueling. Long workdays, very little sleep, patients, and being ordered around like the good little grunts they were. There was an element of excitement to it all and Alex was learning. The practical application of it all was a nice transition from the theories he learned in medical school. It was very fast paced but he got used to it after a while. Interestingly enough, Alex was still able to see his girlfriend enough to maintain a solid relationship. Then he began to think about the horror stories that he heard. But they were just that, stories.

Enough time had finally passed. Alex was now a house officer. He was placed in a hospital not too far from where he lived and he was in a department that was in line with his interests. It was as close to perfect as could be. The only drawback was the 24-hour shifts. Alex didn't know how to prepare for shifts that long. "How could a human work for 24 hours straight" he questioned, "but there must be a way to make it work." For every 24 hour shift he worked, he had the next two days off. "Plenty of time to recover," he thought.

Work was having a physical and emotional toll on Alex. His 24-hour shifts in the ICU (Intensive Care Unit) were exhausting. There was no telling what the day would bring. Some days were manageable and other days were downright insane. During the insane shifts, it would be difficult to squeeze a moment in to eat but that wasn't even the tough part. It was the hopelessness of the cases that was difficult for Alex. Most of the patients in the ICU were in terrible condition. The percentage of patients in the ICU who died was high. For Alex, there was something about trying to save people who were near death and watching them die week after week that was eating away at his soul.

The unexpected effects were the worst. He would have deja vu from being in the ICU when he was younger and his grandfather died. It brought up painful memories at sporadic periods that made it difficult for him to be his best while on his shifts. And the two days off were hardly restful for Alex. The day after a 24-hour shift was almost non-existent. Alex would collapse in bed and do nothing besides sleep and eat. "A body was not meant to function like this," he would grumble. The day before his return to the hospital was mental warfare.

He tried to convince himself to do some healthy activities like spending time with his girlfriend or friends, going to the gym, or simply cleaning the house. He typically resigned that mental battle to playing video games and watching Netflix in the darkness of his room. He did this all day while shuddering at the thought of returning to work.

Alex's dream job was turning out to be more of a nightmare. All the countless hours of school and hard work had brought him to this point, yet he was hating every minute of it. He began fantasizing about doing anything other than being a doctor. What got to him was the lack of control he had over his life. So he decided that he would attempt to move to another department but he was blocked at each turn. This frustrated him to no end.

For Alex, there were two choices: quit or power through until he could figure something out. He was not ready to resign from his dream because he had come too far and he also had bills to pay. However, he admitted to himself that something had to change. "There is not much that I can control while on my shift," he thought. The change needed to be made outside of work. He did not think he could stomach too big a change, so he decided to take it step by step. The first change was to hit the gym at least twelve hours after his shift ended no matter what. He rationalized that this would be the best period to hit the gym. He asked his close friend to be his gym buddy so that he was less likely to cancel.

The first few gym sessions were rough especially when he had a tough work shift. It was an uphill battle at times and he came very close to quitting and staying in bed. But his gym buddy was very persistent and would not hear any excuse from Alex. Eventually, the gym days became more enjoyable. The workouts help release stress and they did wonders for his sleep. He found that he would be more energized when he started his shift and the crash was not as bad afterward (though it was still pretty rough).

Stage two of his change included taking a trip somewhere outdoorsy every two weeks. He became a pasty-skinned individual due to the little contact he got from the sun. He decided to rally his friends and girlfriend and organized a short hike. "This was just what the doctor ordered," he thought chuckling at his joke.

On the hike, Alex soaked in all the elements of the environment and the laughter from his friends was well-needed. He realized this was the first time in a long while that he was not quaking mentally at the thought of his next 24-hour shift. He was at ease and although he was pretty tired when he got home that evening, he was refreshed in more than just a physical way. During his shift, he was more alert and aware. It was as if a weight had been lifted. He was feeding his soul and it was making a difference.

Over the next few months, Alex kept adding new activities and alternating them week by week. And although his work environment did not change, he found that he was more physically and emotionally ready to deal with work. On his off days, he chose socializing over hiding in a dark room. His friends and girlfriend were happy to see him more frequently. Things weren't perfect but they were better.

***

There are times where you are unable to make impactful changes to your external environment. Putting all your energy into changing the things that you cannot control tends to bring you frustration. That frustration can escalate into anxiety, anger, or depression. These negative emotions when prolonged can thrust you into dark places. When you focus on what you can control and change, you empower yourself which helps to produce a positive internal environment that will radiate outward.

Not Just a Haircut

Affirmation: I take full accountability for my actions.

The long drives we're becoming a real hassle. "It was just a haircut," James thought. He wanted to get a nice affordable trim somewhere not too far from where he lived. His previous barber was located too far which didn't bother him initially because he wanted to support his friend. However, it was becoming a task to travel such a distance for just a haircut. He posted a status on his social media: "Looking for a new barber. Must be clean, timely, and situated in the north."

His old buddy from high school quickly jumped into his chat. He told him that he should check out his barber but only if he was serious. James found the portion of the message "only if he was serious" a bit strange. "It's just a barbershop, it's not that serious," he thought. Still, he requested the barber's information.

The barbershop was called Swagg Elite Artistry and run by a barber named Keron. James found their page and made an appointment. The appointment page was pretty ludicrous to James because there was a disclaimer that popped out before the appointment could be booked. It stated that if you were fifteen minutes late for the appointment, it would be canceled. "Fair enough, " James thought. But the note continued to state that you would have to pay the full price of the haircut that was missed when you arrive at your next appointment.

"How extreme," James thought. "How does he get any clients with that type of added pressure? At any rate, James made his decision to try the barber. On the day of the haircut, he was nervous about arriving late and potentially having to pay the late fee. This thought encouraged him to leave fifteen minutes earlier than he had originally planned, which was not typical for him. When he arrived, he expected that he would have to wait just like in other barbershops but was shocked to find out that Keron was ready with an open chair. "I guess it's a good thing that I arrived on time," he thought.

The barbershop had a classic look and feel to it. The place was spotless, not even a hair on the ground. And all the tools were well-organized on the shelf. Keron gave off a very professional feel, almost like he was running a corporation. He gave off a no-nonsense, educated, and serious about his business type of aura. Even Keron's attire was quite professional. His apron and clothes matched the aesthetic of the shop.

"How strange," James thought. He was accustomed to unkempt barbershops that were unkempt, blasting loud uncensored music. Of course, a long wait no matter if an appointment was made or not.

James was enthralled by the conversation that ensued. They chatted about why Keron ran his business the way he did, how the late fee gets him the clientele that he wanted, and how he had been running his business like this for years much to the disbelief of many of his friends and family. They told him it would never work and that he was a fool. He then asked James what was a goal he was working on.

James was taken aback by this question because he came for a haircut and the small talk was starting to feel more like a coaching session. Nevertheless, James answered. "Well, I work at the bank currently and it's okay. Recently I had an idea for a great book, but I don't know anything about writing books. I wasn't exactly the best when it came to English writing in school but I am looking into it," said James. Keron was impressed by the thought of writing a book and encouraged James. He told him that he was looking forward to the next update on his book journey then finished up the haircut.

The haircut was excellent, but it was the conversation that stuck with James more than anything else. Later, James decided to book another appointment. James stuck with the same barber for about two months, then he began noticing a change in himself. For one, he became a real stickler for arriving on time for everything. He began leaving fifteen minutes earlier to all his appointments. He had not been late to anything in weeks. He even began coming down on his friends for being late to events and keeping him waiting. "It's funny how the fear of paying a late fee spilled over into other aspects of my life," he thought.

Also, James felt hard-pressed to bring updates of progress to each visit. He did not want to sit on Keron's barbering chair and not have an update about how his life was progressing. This spurred him on to start writing his book. Four chapters in and he was making considerable headway. Maybe he would not have begun writing his book as quickly as if he hadn't started seeing Keron for haircuts. There was also something very therapeutic about talking through your week. His haircut appointments were almost like a mini counseling session. Keron had a real knack for getting James to talk about the day-to-day things that were troubling him and that he was attempting to ignore. The barbershop started to feel less like a barbershop and more like an all-in-one shop for mental health, coaching, and self-care.

One day James had a very important job interview. The job title would allow for more flexibility so that he could spend more time writing and the pay was better than his current job. He booked an appointment for a haircut right before the interview because a fresh haircut made him feel more confident and that's what he wanted to shine through in the interview. He began getting ready but obsessed compulsively over what he would wear to the interview. He wanted to make a tremendous first impression. This caused him to run late. He thought he would make it to the haircut appointment on time.

Unfortunately, he arrived twenty minutes late but he figured it was his first late appointment so it should not be an issue. When he arrived late, he was dismayed by the news that he would be unable to get a haircut. James began fuming internally. He said, "but there is no one here." Keron became steely-eyed and told him that the next appointment would arrive in ten minutes and it was not worth shifting his entire appointment schedule. The barber also reminded James that he still had to pay for this missed appointment. James paid and left in a horrible mood.

With an unkempt head of hair and a sour attitude, the interview did not go well. James was so wrapped in anger by what happened that he could not focus. He tripped up his words and did not stick to the answers he rehearsed. He left that interview knowing there was no way he would get that job. He blamed Keron and his ridiculous system for his poor interview and decided to never return.

One week later and James still had not gotten a haircut and it would be an understatement to say that he was long overdue for one. James decided to try the barbershop near his office. He walked in and asked how long the wait was. The barber told him there were three people in front of him. Annoyed by the long wait time, he had no choice but to take a seat and bide his time. The place was filthy and the couch he sat on was old and worn. James felt uncomfortable and the loud blasting music was not helping. He put on his headphones and zoned out as he waited.

Finally, it was his turn. He got up and took a seat. However, the barber did not start immediately. He began chatting with a patron that walked in. They began drinking a beer and continued talking loudly. James' agitation grew. He waited for so long and now the barber seemed to have had no care in the world. When the barber finally began cutting his fair, he was still holding the beer and loudly chatting with the other patron. James could smell the beer on his breath. The whole situation enraged him.

He would have walked out if not for the fact that he had waited so long already. James said nothing the entire time and once it was all over, paid the barber and flew out the door. "I'm never going back there!" he fumed. He thought about his experience with Keron and noted the extreme difference in service. He felt it was time to forget his misdirected anger and go back to Keron's barbershop.

After booking an appointment two weeks later, James walked into the barbershop timidly. He sat on the chair but Keron behaved normally as though James had never left. James relaxed and it was business as usual until the barber asked how the book was going. He shamefully reported that he had not written anything in the past few weeks. Keron gave him a disappointing glare and told him that he better change that. James could feel himself mentally getting back in line. His barber/coach/counselor was back and it was time for James to get back to work.

Three years later and James continues his haircuts with Keron. Much has changed. James left his job and was now a full-time writer. With three books already under his belt, he was already halfway through writing the fourth. He looks forward to his weekly haircuts with Keron and makes sure to bring good news to each meeting as they always laugh and talk through the entire haircut.

**

Guidance, empowerment, and stability can come from an unexpected place. Try to be open to what is new, stay near to those that make you feel empowered and inspired. Pride can hold you back. What sometimes lies on the other side of pride are your dreams. Surround yourself with people who will embolden you to live above your prideful ways. When there are more and more people rooting for your success, you experience a greater degree of responsibility to perform. And if you have missteps along your journey, try not to be so quick to blame others. Take responsibility for your actions and be willing to say when you have messed up. That is maturity. That is growth.

Take a breath

Affirmation: If God is for me, who can be against me.

"Ugh, I hate this job!" Jeremy shouted. Screaming like this was his morning ritual. Every morning he lamented about having to wake up to commute to his "prison," as he called it. He hyped himself up each morning to muster the mental fortitude to make it through the long day. Some mornings this process would take five minutes and other mornings it would take one hour. Of course, this affected his ability to arrive at work on time.

Once at work, the inner and outer turmoil would rise to a higher level. Jeremy sat at his desk and stared at the mountain of work before him and glared at his supervisor who was noticeably irate because Jeremy had arrived late once again. Unbothered and uncaring, he got to work.

Jeremy wasn't always like this. He had dreams of becoming a lawyer. He was even enrolled in law school at one point. However, the stress of law school brought on a mental meltdown which came on during a critical exam period.

With low funds and very little support from his family, Jeremy relinquished his dream and settled for a desk job while he figured out his life. He had responsibilities and he could not sit around all day doing anything. He placed a time limit on his episode at this new job. Three years he told himself. Fast forward four and a half years and he had become a shell of his former self. He saw his life as a concoction of bitterness, resentment, and negative emotions. The bleakness of each day melded into the next.

Jeremy's mother was concerned by his consistently negative demeanor and insisted that he listens to an audiobook called *The Power of Positive Thinking*. She chose an audiobook quite strategically. She knew Jeremy would claim to have no time to sit and read but he could listen to an audiobook during his commute to work in the mornings. With his new audiobook, Jeremy would listen to the audiobook for at least twenty minutes a day.

He chuckled as he listened to the audiobook. It sounded very much unbelievable. "It can never be this easy," he thought. The book talked about how changing your thoughts can somehow make the external world more bearable. "Complete trash!" he uttered. He thought about his reality—his failure as a law student, the job he hated, how miserable he felt each day, and his lack of direction. Jeremy couldn't imagine how things could change and had long accepted that this was just how life was.

Two weeks later, he finished the audiobook and went through his days as though he had never listened to it. A week later, he was accosted by his manager. Nothing new, but this was especially embarrassing because it was done quite publicly. Embarrassed by what his co-workers must have thought about him, he found a secluded area of the office to finish out the workday and to avoid the judging eyes of his co-workers. Soon enough, Jeremy became distracted and began fiddling with his phone. He came across the audiobook he finished a few days back and decided to listen anew.

The section he played spoke about simple activities one could do to feel better about oneself. Jeremy was down and out at that moment so decided to try the exercises. If this "mumbo-jumbo," as he termed it, could make him feel better, he thought why not give it a try. One of the exercises was to say aloud an affirmation of your choosing for five uninterrupted minutes. The author explained that this exercise is useful when you are feeling exceptionally low. A devout(ish) Catholic, Jeremy decided to go with the biblical affirmation of "If God is for me, who can be against me (Romans 8:31)."

Jeremy repeated the affirmation for five minutes straight. He even closed his eyes as he did it. After five minutes had passed, he had to admit that he was feeling a little bit better. Though his mood had lightened Jeremy still was not ready to face his co-workers. He was, however, ready to get back to work as his reality seemed less crushing.

Now, whenever Jeremy felt the negativity creeping in, he immediately separated himself from the situation and took five minutes to say his affirmations. It had become a go-to tool to calm himself down. He continued to listen to the audiobook in hopes of internalizing more of the techniques. As time passed, he added more affirmations and began saying what he was grateful for daily. These actions brought a level of inner peace that he had not felt before. He still hated his job and loathed his supervisor, but he felt less inner turmoil. What was great was that he became less likely to explode when he got upset at work. He would simply take a breath and say his affirmations to the puzzled expressions of his co-workers. Though changes were incremental, over time, they had made a sizable impact upon Jeremy.

***

Sometimes we try to power through the problems in our lives. When we have no strategy for dealing with our problems, they are made worse. Positive affirmations and expressions of gratitude can have a tremendous effect on your emotional state when going through life's woes. Create your own affirmations and say what you are grateful for each day for whatever amount of time you are comfortable with. It may seem insignificant at first but it can have a life-altering impact when done consistently.

Yuh Mad or What!?

Affirmation: My mental health is important. I nurture it daily.

They say your life flashes before your eyes before you die. Sabrina thought she was about to die but her life surely did not flash before her eyes. Time slowed to a crawl. She was completely inverted and she could see her hair flowing in front of her and watched as her phone slammed onto the roof of the car. The vehicle made three more revolutions before slamming to a halt. She then fell unconscious.

She awoke in a hospital bed with an IV attached to her arm and throbbing pain in her head and her leg. She felt dazed and unable to focus. Her vision was blurry and she began panicking. At that moment the nurse ran over and began calming her down. He explained that she had been in a terrible car accident but she would be okay. Feeling overwhelmed, she began to cry.

A few minutes later, Sabrina was comforted by the warm embrace of her mother who had entered the room. Her mother asked her what she remembered from the accident. Sabrina closed her eyes and tried to remember. " I remember Jason and I were heading down the highway. We were almost home and then . . . OH YESS!!!," she exclaimed suddenly. "A car broke the red light and hit us! The next thing I knew we were flipping. It was terrifying. I thought I was going to die!" She began crying again. Her mother got up and hugged her again. "Where is Jason!?" Sabrina asked frantically. Her mom told her that he was okay and only had a concussion. It was clear to Sabrina that her leg was broken, as was evident by the cast on her left leg, and her mother explained that she suffered a concussion. Sabrina was happy to be alive.

Sabrina had to take things slow for the next few weeks as she grew accustomed to wearing a cast. She received time off of work and her professors postponed her exams to a later date. She was thankful for the special treatment. However, what was not so great were the frequent flashbacks from the accident. While doing normal activities such as brushing her teeth, she'd be interrupted by these unwanted memories. One minute everything would be all good and the next she was zoning out. A memory of the other car colliding with her car would take hold. Even though it was just a memory, the emotions it invoked were very real and quite intense.

The memories even occurred when she slept. "Those were the worst episodes," she thought to herself. She would wake up screaming and drenched in sweat. The entire household would be awake after that. Sabrina would sometimes be too fearful to go back to sleep. She was constantly on edge. Her friends and boyfriend wanted to be there for her but the more they tried to comfort her, the more agitated she would get. She would inadvertently snap at them angrily even though she wanted to accept their comfort. They were being slowly pushed away and Sabrina began feeling more and more isolated from everyone around her.

It was all getting to be too much. Soon she would have to return to work. It was going to be a mess if she returned to her current state. "What can I do?" she wondered. She decided to do some web searches on what she was experiencing. Post-Traumatic Stress Disorder kept coming up. She was a bit relieved to see that what she was experiencing was normal after an accident. She went down the rabbit hole of information to find out what she could do. The articles she read were useful but it appeared she needed to speak to a therapist to get the help she needed.

She approached her mom about seeing a therapist. Her mom scoffed and said, "Not my child. My daughter is not mad in the head. You don't need to talk to anybody. You will be fine with time baby. You're not crazy." Sabrina was surprised by her mom's attitude towards therapy. She could not understand how her mother could respond that way especially after the weeks of suffering Sabrina had experienced. Sadly, it wasn't just her mother. She ran the idea by her close friends and family. Each time she was met with skepticism. "What was so wrong with seeing a therapist?" she speculated. It felt like she stepped on a taboo land mine, but she was determined to get better.

Luckily for her, Sabrina had a friend who was a personal development coach and understood her situation. She referred a therapist to Sabrina and so she took it upon herself to set up a visit. The first session with the therapist put things in perspective. She felt less like an alien going through some type of unknown affliction. The therapist talked about how common PTSD was and expanded on the information that Sabrina found online. The therapist gave her a few activities that she could use when she felt an episode coming on. They set another appointment to assess the changes.

The appointments were expensive but the activities that the therapist recommended were useful. Sabrina was seeing results. Talking through the traumatic experience with her therapist also helped to diminish the frequency of the episodes and feel less on edge. After a few weeks, Sabrina was beginning to feel more like herself. Therapy was having such a positive impact on her life that she wanted to share her experience with others.

She decided to do a few short videos talking about the accident, her PTSD, and what therapy was like. She honestly thought that she would get negative comments from people telling her that she was weak or mad in the head, but she was pleasantly surprised. There was an outpouring of support in the comments under the videos. A few people even expressed their mental health challenges. It seemed Sabrina had inspired others to speak up.

Some of her followers asked about resources and asked tough questions on what they should do with their particular problem. Sabrina was not ready for all that and she was no professional so she could not give them suitable advice. Instead, she decided to talk to her therapist about it. She wanted to help those in need but she needed to figure out a proper way.

Her therapist shared free and paid resources and offered up numerous books she could read so she could be more knowledgeable about the topic. Sabrina's friend who was the personal development coach was very impressed by her passion to help the people who had reached out to her. He suggested that she start a non-governmental organization (NGO) focused on mental health. A light bulb went off in Sabrina's head as those words left her friend's lips. "That's a great idea!" she shouted.

Her friend provided some general information that she would need to create the organization. Soon after, Sabrina started planning out how she could start. She felt getting her new venture up and running would be a tremendous amount of work. But the thought of helping those who were in a similar position to her, or even worse, made her feel inspired to get it done.

Four years had passed. Sabrina's NGO has been in operation for two and a half years and has made great strides to educate and demystify the topic of mental health. She has therapists and useful resources available for anyone who needs them. In its short life, Sabrina's NGO has helped educate hundreds of people on their mental health needs.

***

Take care of your mental health. There is a stigma surrounding mental health where people are labeled as mad, weak, or crazy. It's completely okay to seek help. It's completely okay to not be okay all the time. You do not need to suffer in silence and isolation. The first step to addressing your mental health is asking for help and trusting in the process. Let our generation be the generation to eradicate that negative label for something so important. We can be the generation to foster an environment that encourages and normalizes mental health wellness. This will help ease the anxiety of so many and help save the lives of those who are struggling with their mental health.

An Ironic Turn of Events

Affirmation: I am innovative, progressive, and dynamic.

"How do you expect us to get this done in time? You guys are making quick decisions and setting targets for new projects but don't have a full understanding of the workload that you put on us," Sarah argued. She was livid. The start of a new quarter and her manager was up to the same ridiculous requests. "They always do this," she thought to herself. The managers decided on what the next big project was, and for this campaign, what they were proposing was on another level of difficulty.

Sarah was tired of not having her voice heard so she gradually became more and more vocal and less and less anxious about the repercussion. "They want us to work like dogs but when we don't hit their predetermined targets, we (the junior staff) are the ones that are punished," she fussed. She was at her wit's end. "What is more agitating is that they expect so much out of us, but they won't entertain our feedback or ideas." Her most recent suggestion outlining a two-day work-from-home policy was shut down.

Sarah had read *The 4-Hour Workweek* by Tim Ferriss and was intrigued by the work-from-home formula that he laid out. She recently gave birth to a beautiful baby boy and wanted to find a way to work from home so that she could be with her son more often. The majority of the activities at the office could be done remotely. The presentation that she put together for her manager measured her productivity on the days she was allowed to work from home versus working at the office. It was laced with productivity statistics. From the data it was clear she was more productive at work. The presentation also included ways to track employees' productivity while working remotely, resources that would make the transition seamless, and the expected benefits to staff satisfaction which would roll over into work efficiency.

Sarah was impressed by her work but unfortunately her bosses were not. Their main argument was that there was no reason to change anything because the business worked well as is. "Works well for you maybe," she retorted in her mind. They uttered a sentence that completely turned Sarah off and made her realize this was an unwinnable fight: "This is how we've always done things and will continue to do so." That was it. The fight was over. Sarah considered quitting based on how things were run in the organization, but what happened next, no one could have imagined.

A global pandemic affected the entire world. Covid-19 was running rampant worldwide and it made its way to her tropical twin-island, Trinidad & Tobago. Cases began popping up all around the country and in an instant, the country was on lockdown. Sarah's company was forced to consider work from home based on lockdown protocol. Now, what was otherwise thought impossible, was seriously being considered. Sarah could not help but laugh at the situation. The same ideas she pitched only weeks earlier were now the model the company was using to implement work from home.

Suddenly, Sarah was a highly sort after expert in the organization. She was invited to a manager's-only meeting to explain how to roll out her work from home policy. However, handholding was needed. The technology was new to most of the managers and they needed to understand it fully to use it properly. Sarah was their go-to girl for all things virtual, remote productivity tracking, and policy creation. The tables had turned dramatically. She used her newfound leverage to negotiate a pay raise for herself because she was doing more work and managing other employees as a result. The company had no choice but to give her what she wanted or they risked falling behind their competitors as they scrambled to find someone new to replace her.

It was disheartening to see what the pandemic was doing to her countrymen and women. Though for Sarah, there was a silver lining. She continued to help the different managers and teams to adjust to the new normal. Additionally, with her new position and more power, she was able to lobby on behalf of the junior staff for more reasonable conditions. Even though they were all working from home, there was still the potential that they could be overworked. With no defined working hours, it would be easy for a manager to call, request work, or send urgent emails at all hours and pressure the junior staff to act immediately. Sarah was ready to help with this new problem and was in the right position to do so.

Once the pandemic was over and normalcy returned to people's lives, Sarah was recognized for her abilities. It did not take long for her to be elevated to a management position. She continued to create a bridge between the junior and senior staff while keeping the goals of the company at the forefront. Under her care, her department routinely generated and executed new and innovative ideas.

Sarah fostered an "open door" policy whereby she encouraged staff to bring forward their ideas for how the unit could operate more productively. No idea was too big or too small to be considered. As a result, her unit pumped out idea after idea with the backing of most, if not all the unit staff, because everyone had a hand in the creation process.

***

It should not take a massive problem like a dip in sales or a global pandemic for the older generations to see your worth. Always be aware of your potential and never let anyone cast a shadow over your brilliance. You add value but you also need to know what you are doing is more than just a job. What's the deeper meaning? Who are you helping? How will you change the world? Never change your way of thinking or perspective based on your work environment. Because within you lies the potential to do great and innovative things. All that's left for you to do is to find a way to express that internal potential externally.

For Your Page

Affirmation: I am open to all life's opportunities.

Kayla wondered if this was what it was like during the great depression. The fear and uncertainty she felt week in and week out was debilitating. She was new to her job which meant she would be the first one out the door if things took a turn for the worst.

Covid-19 had arrived. This great pandemic was causing lockdowns the world over, and as a result, economies slowed down and jobs were lost. "We were not immune in our little island paradise," she thought.

Kayla didn't particularly like her job but it paid the bills and kept her parents off her back. She would send out resumes in preparation for what was to come. The day finally came that the company she worked for began laying off employees. She was surprised that she wasn't part of the first wave to be let go but her name got called. With no job, Kayla became depressed and dejected. She had little motivation to do anything.

The days dragged on. With the country on lockdown, most places that provided entertainment were closed. Gathering in groups larger than ten was prohibited and social interaction was at an all-time low due to social distancing. The year 2020 was a big let-down. All Kayla could do was go online. Outside of the more popular platforms like Instagram and Twitter, Kayla found herself joining a newish video platform called Tik Tok. The platform's popularity surged during the lockdown. Not surprisingly, with so many people stuck at home, new users were flocking to the platform in the millions and Kayla was one of them.

Bored one afternoon she decided to make her first video for Tik Tok. She re-created the timeless scene from Lion King where Simba is born and held in the air by Rafiki for all the animals below to see. The twist was that she used a puppy and hilarious clothing to re-enact it. At one point it seemed she dropped Simba (the puppy) accidentally into the animals below. Although the video was simple, it took a considerable amount of time to edit. Kayla was not a video editor but she enjoyed making the video. She was also shocked at how well the video did when she posted it on Tik Tok. She was getting thousands of views for a video idea she birthed one boring afternoon.

Kayla continued making videos. She re-created segments of iconic Caribbean shows, old-time cartoons, and took part in all the fun viral videos that were trending at that time. Before she knew it, she was cranking out three or four videos a day. Her sisters and brothers would join in the fun and she even got her cousin to help edit the videos. Her cousin dabbled in video editing and needed a distraction from virtual school. Seemingly overnight, she became Tik Tok famous. Her videos were getting between 50,000 to sometimes 100,000 views. One even got up to 250,000 views. She did this all while having fun with her siblings.

One day a friend asked if he could place one of his juice products in the background as she did one of her videos. He was willing to pay her for the placement. Kayla realized that she could make money off of this. She began thinking about the best approach to monetizing her videos. She looked up all the big local brands, got contacts for their marketing people, and emailed as many of them as she could each day. She kept up the video production and partnered with a video studio with professional cameras and a green screen.

The requests were pouring in. For every ten emails she sent, she got favorable replies from two or three. The brands were impressed with her engagement numbers, and most wanted her to simply place their product somewhere in the video. "This is easy money," she thought.

With all the money she was making, she decided to register a business and turn her videos into something legitimate. She got an agent to filter her requests and make deals on her behalf. She invested her profits into constructing a home studio and she even hired an assistant. Who knew something born out of boredom would have transformed into a business idea that could generate income in a rough financial period?

***

It's an amazing thing when you find an outlet to express your creativity to the world. And if it helps pay the bills, that's even better. In a time where anything is possible and you can reach thousands, even millions in minutes, the sky's the limit. It's up to you to create your own path to prosperity. So don't place a ceiling over your possibilities. Keep your options open, and when what is possible suddenly becomes real, work tirelessly to produce amazing results.

80/20 Warrior

Affirmation: I focus on my top priorities.

Fresh out of insurance agent training Justin was ready to make his mark as an insurance agent. He was excited by the vision of the company. Although a new agent, he saw himself more as a financial change agent. His goal was to help his clients make better financial decisions. If that meant they bought insurance from him, great, if not, it did not matter once they were in a better place financially. As a new agent, he bubbled with enthusiasm. He planned to put his best foot forward. He was well aware that this journey would not be an easy one, but he was willing to outwork anyone to prove himself.

Justin used any means available to get the word out that he was now an insurance agent in hopes of getting clients. Firstly, he spoke to all his close friends and family members. He then jumped on all the different social media platforms: LinkedIn, Facebook, Instagram, and Twitter. He frequently posted good advice and educated his followers on how they could increase their financial literacy. He talked to anyone about anything dealing with money. This placed him right in the middle of many heated discussions happening via Facebook comments by people who were spreading misinformation. Between the sales meetings, social media, and administrative work, it did not take long for Justin to feel overwhelmed.

"How am I supposed to keep up this pace? I am exhausted," he thought to himself. He also felt like he wasn't making much headway. Sure, he was getting sales here and there but for the considerable effort he was putting in, he was expecting way more results. He ignored his thoughts of "distraction" as he called them and doubled down his efforts. He began direct messaging people on all his platforms. He wanted to reach out to as many people as possible so he wrote a sales script that he copied and pasted as quickly as he could to as many people as he could. The strategy was extremely time-consuming. And for some reason, most people did not reply. Justin was puzzled. "Do these people not care for the future?" he wondered.

He kept pushing and pushing and pushing. The line between work time and personal time became blurred. Eventually, his free time dwindled. He was also unsure of what work tasks to focus on and in what order. His to-do list was growing longer by the day and no matter how much work he did, he could not curtail it. Many tasks—such as following up with prospective clients and his administrative work—remained on his to-do list for weeks to his dismay. The pressure intensified by the day and Justin felt himself on the brink of burnout.

The company would bring an expert in for training each quarter. The quarterly training sessions were typically focused on sales to help the unit perform better. They were mandatory and Justin grumbled that he did not have time to waste on training when he had so much work piling up. Jarrod, the trainer, wore a yellow jacket with a white shirt with horizontal yellow stripes, light yellow jeans, and yellow shoes. "I wonder what this guy's favorite color is?" Justin joked. But little did Justin know; Jarrod would change his day-to-day actions forever.

Jarrod wasted no time in his presentation. He began outlining all the negative actions novice sales reps take. The list was lengthy and to Justin's embarrassment, many of the actions he did fell on that list. The list contained actions such as direct messaging followers with an impersonal message, not having a prioritized list of actions each day, working yourself to death, etc. Justin sunk into his seat to hide from the imaginary giant spotlight that Jarrod was shining on him. He felt attacked by Jarrod's words.

Jarrod explained something called the Pareto Principle. Justin never heard of it so he leaned forward in his seat so he could hear every word. The principle suggested that 80% of our results come from 20% of our actions and that the inverse was also true, 80% of our actions yield 20% of our results. Jarrod explained that most new sales reps focus too much on the 80% of actions that don't give them the results they want. Explaining further, he said that a sales rep should take note of their daily actions and quantify which of these actions produce the most bang for their buck. Jarrod also highlighted that the Pareto Principle went deeper than just sales. It was a life lesson.

Jarrod proposed a challenge to his audience. He asked them to list out all the actions that they do on a typical day. "Quantify which of these activities yields the most results and circle those high yielding actions," he instructed. "From there, it would be easier to prioritize those high-priority actions over everything else." Justin immediately thought that Jarrod's request was immensely difficult. "How could I prioritize some actions over others? The other actions would never get done and then what?" he thought to himself. Jarrod continued, "All the simple actions that take up a lot of your time, that anyone could do, hire a virtual assistant to get it done for you." Jarrod affirmed that with the sales rep focusing on the 80% of activities that yield few results, the sales reps could now focus on the 20% that yield the higher results. With an increase in results, the rationale was that the sales rep should be able to pay the virtual assistant.

Justin had to sit and digest Jarrod's words for a moment. He admitted that they made sense. He was drowning in work but not all the work he needed to do himself. He could outsource the social media management and admin work to someone else, while he focused on making sales. He also realized that with more time he could put more effort into building relationships with people online as opposed to sending scripted messages. He began making sense out of his current predicament.

After the talk Justin made changes that transformed his sales. He made a priority list of the three most important activities he had to complete before lunch each day. He also made a list of all the simple and time-consuming tasks and hired a virtual assistant part-time to do it for him. Things didn't always go according to plan every day, for instance, he did not communicate instructions to the virtual assistant effectively at the beginning which caused errors. But they were minor. He also did not always finish his most important activities before lunch, but his results were staggering.

Justin's sales had increased by almost 120%. Not only that, but he had more free time. He began using the 80/20 rule in his life also. Focusing on the tasks that gave him the most bang for his buck and enjoying the freedom that came with it. He received the rookie of the year award for his soaring sales numbers and for being at the top of his unit in sales each quarter.

***

Success doesn't always come by simply working hard. You must be able to place yourself in the best position to get the results you want. This means being strategic about how you prioritize your tasks so that you don't run around like a headless chicken. Focus on the 20% that will yield the greatest results. Once you take note of your most important tasks, use them as your shield against anything or anyone that seeks to distract you. Your achievements are waiting on the other side of your determination. Stay focused, prioritize, and get results.

The Songbird's Crisis

Affirmation: I am the architect of my life. No situation will deter my greatness.

Some people are blessed with the ability to draw or are naturally good at sports. Nkese, however, was blessed with a beautiful voice. Her melodic voice was apparent ever since she was a little girl. She was front and center in her school's choir and she was no stranger to talent shows or karaoke outings. When she reached high school her aunt asked her to sing at her wedding and paid her for it. "Who knew that singing in the shower could lead to some cash in my pocket," she thought.

As time passed, Nkese began thinking about her future. "Singing is fun and I make some money out of it but I need to start thinking about a serious career." With no shortfall of intelligence, she decided on working towards becoming a doctor. Medicine was always interesting to her. But it was natural medicine that appealed to her, not so much conventional medicine. She spent hours researching where she could learn natural medicine. Her effort eventually paid off when she found what looked like the perfect school. There was only one problem: the school was in Beijing, China, halfway across the globe.

Where most people saw an impossible obstacle, Nkese saw a challenge to overcome. She began taking introductory classes in Chinese and satisfying all the requirements to be accepted into the school. The chips were lining up nicely. She was making considerable headway on starting her dream. By the time she had achieved a conversational level of Chinese, it was time for her to make the long journey to China.

China was a completely different culture than her homeland of Trinidad and Tobago. Beaches were replaced with tall buildings and permanently neon-lit structures. The slow-paced carefree island time was replaced with the cramped hustle and bustle of China. It was different and amazing. She learned so much in her time there. Natural medicine was everything she had hoped for and much much more! It was heaven albeit an oft-overwhelming heaven due to her studies.

Due to her being a well performing student Nkese was offered partial scholarships from the school in Beijing which helped to pay off some of her fees, but the scholarships were not enough. One day in a panicked frenzy, she started working out how she could acquire the money to stay in school. She began teaching English to Chinese children on the side, which to her surprise paid a considerable amount. It even crossed her mind to quit school and teach English for a few years. But as soon as those thoughts arrived, they then left.

An ad offering voice coaching repeatedly popped up during her time in Beijing and this spurred her on to reach out to the individual to test her pipes. "Singing could be a great avenue for me to earn some income," she thought. The coaching proved fruitful as her singing voice was revived. On top of it all, she had built a close relationship with her coach. Impressed with Nkese, her coach referred her to a band that was seeking a singer. "That's perfect," Nkese thought.

Nkese met with the band and sang a few tunes for them and the rest was history. On the weekdays she continued to attend her classes and studied or taught English in the evenings. On the weekends she performed or practiced with the band. The band's popularity grew quickly thanks to Nkese. There was a great deal of appeal for Nkese because she was from the Caribbean and there weren't many Caribbean singers in China with a voice like hers.

Her time in China was coming to an end. It was a thrilling few years. After graduation she decided to remain in China for another year. She took on more teaching hours and more singing gigs. She was making a lot of money and her outlook for her future was beginning to change. She thought about shelving her plans to become a doctor. Her passion for singing reached a new peak and she wanted to go big. Who knows what could happen? In that year in China, she saved as much as she could and worked her butt off to get as much exposure as she possibly could.

She researched how she could develop herself as an artist and discovered an artist development team based in the UK. A few phone calls and Zoom conversations later, she was considering going to the UK to meet with them. In a funny turn of events, she was put on to a producer through conversations with the artist development team, and although she decided not to train with them, she did build a relationship with the producer. This relationship created an avenue for her to record her singles which had the potential to become a full album.

She returned to Trinidad to make preparations for her UK visit where she would begin recording her songs. She stayed in contact with the producer via virtual meetings as she made preparations, but she noticed the producer's tone changed. Everyone was a bit weary of the environment as Covid-19 was quickly spreading worldwide. Nkese would not let this opportunity slip through her fingers and requested that the timeline for the recordings be moved up. She was willing to leave Trinidad as soon as possible.

With an adjusted schedule, Nkese was on the first flight out of Trinidad. She did not waste any time. Within the first week, she had already recorded four songs. She felt like a star in the making. Then she received some unfortunate news. Trinidad was about to close its borders. If she did not leave immediately, she would not be able to re-enter her own country for who knows how long. She had no choice but to cut the recordings short and return home. She somehow got on the final flight back into Trinidad and self-quarantined at home for a very boring two weeks.

The uncertainty with how long the pandemic would last forced Nkese to give up on returning to the UK to record her other songs. Nkese was crushed. With no plan B and borderline depressed, she also gave up the idea of becoming a doctor. She got the taste of being a singer and she could not let it go. While mindlessly scrolling on social media she saw a post from a close friend about his new book called *The Millennial Mind*, which he recently launched. She was a Millennial and wanted to support her friend, so she called him up to place an order. Within two days she had her copy and began reading.

The stories and lessons within the book were useful. There were points in the book where she felt like her friend's words were talking to her directly. Then she read a portion that struck her at her core:

"Empowerment comes from the acceptance that this is your life. It may not be perfect but it belongs to you. It may not be exactly the way you want it to be and that's okay. No one's life is exactly the way they want it to be and no one is without some level of worry or stress. Even when you achieve the things you want, some new worry will appear and prod you to work towards overcoming it. I would urge you to focus more on what it is exactly that makes you happy. I mean truly happy."

Nkese began crying uncontrollably. She felt like those lines spoke exactly to her current struggle. Everything she worked for was falling apart and she had no options until now. From that point on, she began thinking about what she could do in her home country. She decided then and there that she would become an international crossover artist.

Although Nkese was popular in China, she was challenged by not having a significant social media presence and not knowing many people in the music industry. So she began writing songs, pulling a team together to create music videos, and building her social media presence. She even found an agent. As Trinidad was now on lockdown, she could not perform anywhere and decided instead to go all-in on social media. She ran ads on Youtube, Facebook, and Instagram. She pumped out video after video of her new songs. She was amazed as her popularity slowly grew week after week.

She got overwhelming support from her friends and she was beginning to take off on social media. She still remembered the first time she heard one of her songs on the radio. The pure excitement that coursed through her entire body was exhilarating. It was a lot of work for Nkese but she was seeing traction which motivated her to keep pushing. She could see herself making it big. She smiled every time she thought of the twists and turns that her life took. She was ready to take control and achieve greatness.

With a few years of performing now under her belt, Nkese P, as she was now called, had recorded her fourth studio album. Her fame rose to heights that have garnished her recognition in the Caribbean, the UK, China, and the United States. With a fandom in the hundreds of thousands, Nkese was poised to become an international star.

***

When life throws you for a loop, you have the power to move past whatever challenging situation that you're facing. We have more control over our lives than we often give ourselves credit for. It is so easy to get caught up with the negative things happening around us but doing so relinquishes our power. It distracts us and we lose focus. If you feel like you lack control, regain it by stating all of the things that you feel are within your control. It is through these steady acts of self-empowerment that we rally and begin putting our lives back into place. Remember that positive change starts within before it works its way out.

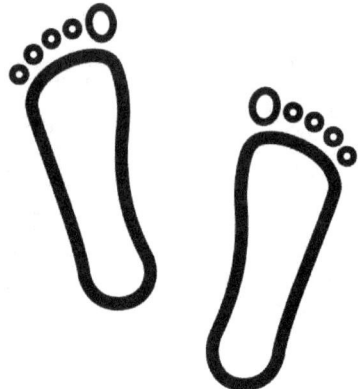

The Stumps Great Journey

Affirmation: My dreams are a gateway into my bright future.

Liselle sat sipping her tea. The weather was pleasantly cool and the air was filled with the aroma of freshly brewed coffee. One day she stumbled upon a cafe on her commute to work and quickly she became a regular on weekends. The cafe was her writing spot. She was working on her third book. Still riding high off of the success of the second book, her publisher had been pushing her to write another. She was content with her life and she began to feel nostalgic about the journey that got her to this point.

a few years earlier

Liselle always had a passion for writing. She was talented but often doubted herself. For her, the stories were never good enough. There was never enough time. There was always something out of line that would disrupt her. Slowly as she grew more senior in her job, her writing fell to the wayside. Her life became a constant rush from one thing to the next. She never felt like she had enough time or money or energy. Her life felt out of order and she badly wanted to regain control.

While commuting to work she was a bit ahead of schedule, so she decided to go in to grab a cup of coffee from a cafe. She noticed a flier advertising a short story competition. The thought of entering this competition made her feel a spark of excitement. "It would be great to start writing again but I don't have time for much of anything," she thought to herself. She snapped a picture of the flier anyway just in case she changed her mind.

Her day went by like most other days, at light speed. It never felt like she had full control over the day's activities but she did her best. The thought of entering the short story competition would not leave her thoughts, however. "I'm not good enough to enter this. I don't have the time. Even if I enter, I wouldn't win," She thought. These thoughts went on and on in her head. The battle was lost before it had even begun.

Just then, she got a call from her mother. They chatted for a moment and suddenly Liselle told her mother about the short story competition. Her mother slightly chuckled at hearing the information. Her mother recalled all the cute short stories that Liselle wrote when she was younger. She reminded her that she had more important things to focus on and that she did not have time to focus on this silly dream. Liselle agreed and they ended the conversation.

Liselle mulled over the conversation a bit. Something stood out to her in that instance. She realized that the way her mother spoke echoed the sentiments in her head. Liselle always found herself thinking that she did not have time and she noticed that her mother said those same words frequently. "It could not be a coincidence, could it? It's not strange to adopt the thought process of our parents. They are the ones that raised us," she thought. She wondered how deep this went and was intrigued by the idea of exploring this realization further.

When she got home that afternoon she decided to make a list of all the common sentences or phrases her parents would say while she was growing up, that had a negative or diminishing undertone. She listed the following:

Her list grew longer and longer. It became clear that Liselle had internalized most of these sentiments. Being subjected to these phrases over the years and subconsciously adding them to her vocabulary, she had unwittingly limited herself. Liselle internalized that in many respects she was not good enough. Doubt and fear became her primary setting. This recognition shook her at her core. She was sad to see how she held herself back. "That's going to stop from today," she declared. But first things first, she needed to enter the short story competition. Liselle stopped telling herself that she didn't have enough time and that she was not good enough. Throughout her day, although hectic, she found time to write. She used her phone or a little notepad in her bag, depending on where she was, to jot down ideas. By the end of the week, she had a few short story ideas to play with. Ultimately, she decided on a short story that would be inspired by what she had experienced over the last couple of days.

Her short story was titled, "The Stumps Great Journey." The story was set in a world where the people with many negative beliefs about themselves experienced a greater magnitude of gravity compared to those who thought more positively about themselves. The more gravity you experienced the more sluggish and less agile you were. In this world, individuals who seemed listless or otherwise affected by more gravity were prejudicially called "the stumps." The stumps were considered lower class and treated poorly. They received the worst jobs, experienced more stress, and due to the greater levels of gravity they experienced, they were shorter than everyone else, hence the name "the stumps."

The story followed a young girl who was a stump who had been experiencing the most intense degree of gravity than any other stump. The story followed her struggles and her fight to achieve a better life. Things changed for the girl when she realized that the intense amount of gravity she was experiencing was influenced by her negative self-beliefs. She had internalized all the negative things she was told about herself by her parents who were stumps themselves. She always thought in this manner, so she did not know any other way of thinking. The only way she could better her standard of living was to envision a better life for herself.

The girl decided to go on a journey of self-discovery. It was a long and arduous journey and along the way, she met many new people. Each new person she met had a positive outlook on life. She learned from them and tried to absorb as much of their positive thinking as she could. She realized that her external experience stemmed from her internal beliefs. She had to re-wire herself.

As her self-image slowly began to change so did her experience of gravity. Day by day, she grew lighter and lighter, more able to move freely and with increased agility. She slowly became nimbler. Her life up to this point, having to move about through more gravity, inadvertently strengthened her legs and back. With a positive outlook on life and a lighter weight around her, she was leagues ahead of those who had not experienced her hardship.

Liselle's short story was truly inspirational! She placed fifth overall in the competition. As a newcomer in the industry. Even though she didn't place, she did catch the attention of one of the newspapers. A journalist was sent to interview her and her story was placed in a section of the paper. The article caught the eye of a local publishing company. They approached Liselle about making her short story into a children's book. She could not believe the opportunity she was presented with.

Liselle snapped out of the memory and continued sipping her tea reminiscing on her journey. It still amazed her to this day how much her words affected how she saw herself and her actions. When she was finally able to begin freeing herself of those negative self-beliefs, she became a more inspired and motivated version of herself, and that person was amazing.

***

We all have limiting beliefs whether big or small. Sometimes we can be consumed by our negative experiences and we accept them as our be-all and end-all. The person that we have become as a result of our past is not the person we will be forever. The truth is that although our limiting beliefs are internalized due to our past experiences and conditioning, we are the only ones who can free ourselves from these beliefs. It starts by understanding that you are not wholly defined by your past, that you're greater than the limiting beliefs you've internalized. You have the ability to do great things. Cultivate positive thoughts about yourself and know that they will take you farther than you've ever imagined.

The Boy Who Cried, Wolf

Affirmation: My words equal my deeds.

"How can you sit here and tell me you love me when you are out here embarrassing me!? Do you think that I am stupid or something? I can see you liking all her pictures," Tishelle screamed. "Babe it's just a 'like'. You are blowing this way out of proportion," Jordan replied. "Oh please! You comment under her pictures with flirty compliments. You keep promising that you won't do these things but clearly you don't mean it. You are not serious about this relationship! If you can't commit fully, I won't be in it with you." Tishelle stormed out.

Jordan thought that Tishelle was being overdramatic. "It's not like I can control the messages that come into my phone and what's wrong with liking a post and commenting under it from time to time." This was not the first time that they had this argument. He promised on multiple occasions that he would stop giving attention to certain women because they clearly had feelings for him. But even though he made the promise, he felt like it was not as big a deal as his girlfriend was making it.

Jordan was a part of his local Rotaract Club, an international community service organization with clubs all over the world. The clubs encourage professional development among their members and each one plans its projects around specific world problems: promoting peace, fighting disease, providing clean water, sanitation, and hygiene, etc. Over the next few weeks, he gave his now ex-girlfriend space and decided to focus on what his club was up to.

The club was working on a big food drive and needed help from all the members. The team lead requested that Jordan assist with delivering the packages on the day of the drive. Jordan agreed happily and promised that he would be on time. The team lead was a bit skeptical because Jordan had a track record of not doing what he said he would do but they needed all the help they could get. Jordan could feel the reluctance of the team lead but reassured her that he was up to the task.

On the morning of the food drive, all the drivers were needed at 7 am. By 7:05 am, Jordan is nowhere to be found. The team lead called Jordan repeatedly but with no response. She was furious and was forced to make do with the drivers on hand. Meanwhile, Jordan was still home asleep. He went out the night before with some of his friends. He rarely gets to see them so he felt he had no choice but to go. He planned to leave early so he could wake up on time for the food drive but he slept right through his alarms.

It was near 8:30 am before Jordan finally woke up. Befuddled, he grabbed his phone and was distraught when he realized what time it was. No time for a shower, he quickly brushed his teeth, changed his clothes, and was out the door. He saw five missed calls from the team lead and knew that he was in trouble. He thought to himself, "Why did these guys have to invite me out last night????" He arrived at the meeting point and rushed out of the car. He was immediately met by the glare of the team lead.

"Do you see the time Jordan!? The other drivers are working double time because of you," she howled. Jordan could only offer up petty excuses. The team lead rolled her eyes and sent him off to help. Jordan wished that she hadn't made such a big scene. He understood that he was late but it wasn't such a big deal where he needed to be embarrassed in front of everyone. He rationalized that it was not his fault. And what was he expected to do, not see his friends?

All the packages were delivered. The club had done great work. The next week the members met to review the project and began planning the next one. Jordan was eager to redeem himself and was ready to commit to whatever the club needed. The club decided on a project to assist Habitat for Humanity. This project would require the club members to assist with building and painting a few houses. The site location was a ways out so carpooling was necessary as many club members did not drive. Jordan immediately volunteered himself to transport a few of the club members.

The group was skeptical as some were still upset at him from his performance at the last project. Jordan was adamant and vocal about his dedication to the group. He insisted that he would put his best foot forward this time. The team lead for this project reluctantly agreed. Jordan was excited to prove himself. Two weeks later and it's the day before the project. Jordan had a long week, and on top of that, his ex-girlfriend has been refusing to return his messages and calls. All he wanted to do is relax at home. He began watching a movie and got a message from the group chat that was created to coordinate the club members he would be transporting. He glanced at the messages but got distracted by the movie, so he did not reply. The next thing he knew, he was an hour into the movie, never bothering to reply. Before long, Jordan had drifted off to sleep.

His alarm woke him up and his first thought was that he did not reply to their messages. He opened up the group chat and saw 100-plus messages. He knew things were bad. "If only I had replied to those messages when I first saw the notifications," he thought to himself. He read through all the messages. Everyone was furious that he was not replying. It seemed that they expected as much from him and had a backup plan from the beginning. They organized another driver knowing that Jordan would drop the ball again. Jordan sent a message in the group apologizing and promptly exited the group fearful of what they would say.

When he arrived at the project, all the members were cold towards him. Ashamed, Jordan kept apologizing. But it was pointless. That evening when he arrived home, he decided to think about his actions. He noticed a pattern. He kept saying he would do things and would only follow through with some of what he said. It happened with his ex-girlfriend and it happened with his club. He noticed that he also did it at work and it was the reason why his relationship with his coworkers was so choppy. It was clear to him that he could not continue on this way.

He knew that his words meant very little. He decided to prove himself through action. He wrote and mailed a letter to his ex-girlfriend. He did not know how else to reach her which is why he went with this old school route. In the letter he expressed how much he cherished the time they spent together, admitting that he was wrong for the way he acted and that he understands why she left. He also stated that he understood if they had no future together. At all the future projects, he did not volunteer himself for any activities because he knew his reputation was in the dirt. But on the day of a project, he would show up early and do as much as he could. He was eager to do anything and often would ask if anyone needed help.

He never got a reply from his ex-girlfriend. His club members continued to treat him coldly, but he was determined to keep working on repairing his reputation no matter how long it took. He became very conscious of what he'd promise to do from that point on and made sure that he did what he said. Although things weren't changing as quickly as he'd like, he took solace in knowing that he was seeing a change in himself. He knew eventually that things would turn around.

———

***

Our words can hold great weight or be as light as a feather, it all depends on how our actions align with our words and how accountable we are for what we say we're going to do. Even if we fall short, be accountable for it and know that empty pride can cost you your reputation. Excuses will only make you look worse.

Our level of accountability abates if we don't do what we say we will do. We must also take full accountability when we make mistakes. Don't pass blame when you are the one who has come up short. Don't allow narcissism and empty pride to cost you your reputation. If you don't produce the results that you promised, then that's on you. Save the excuses because they only make you look worse. Get in the habit of owning up to your mistakes. And know that sometimes mistakes happen because growth is needed.

Airplane Mode

Affirmation: I value and protect my personal time.

Tynika knew what she wanted to be from a young age. In her early years, she came across a social worker when one of her teachers questioned her about an alarming essay she wrote. The essay was an assignment for students to talk about what it's like in their family. Tynika's story included details of her father leaving bruises on her mom's body. The teacher raised her essay as a red flag and notified National Family Services. As a result, a social worker was assigned to her family. The social worker assisted her mother and her entire family through tough times. Tynika's father had an abusive streak. And although he eventually was out of the picture, he left behind a trail of physical and psychological devastation. If not for the help of the social worker, who knows what would have happened to Tynika and her mother. From that experience, Tynika grew fond of the social work profession and knew that this was what she wanted to do with her life.

With a clear mission in mind, Tynika stayed focused and eventually became a social worker herself. An empathetic person by nature, the work seemed to be a good fit for her. She cared for each person as if they were a part of her family. She felt that the work she was doing was important. And a by-product of her dedication meant that she sometimes thought about how she could help her clients after work and even on her days off. At times, thinking about work would affect her sleep. She had a work phone for her clients. She was expected to turn her work phone off on the weekends, but she could never bring herself to do so. Tynika was great at her job although it was putting an enormous strain on her physically and emotionally.

Her personal life was no different. She was always ready to help a friend or family member at a moment's notice. So much so that those closest to her knew all too well that they could call on her at any time and she would be there to help. They were accustomed to Tynika never saying "no" to their requests. Never wanting to let anyone down, Tynika would always reply with a hearty, "Yes, of course. I'll be there ASAP." She experienced an internal joy by being able to help everyone around her solve their problems no matter how big or small.

The look of happiness on the faces of her friends, family, and clients was all that she needed or so she thought. Her inability to say no began taking its toll. Fatigue came gradually and it compounded. Tired after a long day of helping her clients, all Tynika wanted to do was rest her mind and body. In her job, she had begun to feel how high the emotional tax was. But everyone has their limit. Her phone buzzed and it was one of her clients. She answered right away. This client was having an especially hard time and needed to talk. She did not want to rush him off the call because he had been dealing with suicidal thoughts recently and she did not want him to revert to that dark place. The call was long but Tynika was able to get him to a better place.

Before she could even take a breath a friend suddenly called and asked for her assistance with a small project. Tynika was happy to help although she couldn't ignore the immense feeling of fatigue building. She rushed over. Once she was finished assisting her friend, she couldn't help but think that her friend could have done the project herself or called someone else to assist. Nevertheless, Tynika was happy to help. Another friend called and it was an urgent request, of course. Not wanting to let her friend down, Tynika agreed to help. After helping her friend, she was completely worn out and it was well into the evening. She called it a night because she had work in the morning. She laid in her bed and calculated the number of hours of sleep she would get if she fell asleep immediately. No matter how many times she tabulated the number, she knew she was not getting enough sleep. She came to terms with the fact that the next day would be rough and begrudgingly went to bed.

Tynika got up the next morning feeling sluggish and got ready for work. She showed up late for her first appointment of the day. Her client was noticeably upset. These relationships are built on trust and Tynika was breaking that trust by being late. Sometimes it takes months for social workers to build a meaningful relationship with their clients. Tynika was a bit disappointed in herself and carried that weight throughout the rest of the day. Things were rough for her.

When she got home she put both her personal and work phone on airplane mode and took the longest most soothing bath to wash away the troubles of the day. For the first time that day, she felt a bit of relief. She changed, jumped in her bed, and took her phone off of airplane mode. Big mistake. She got an influx of messages all from the same person. Her friend was begging her to help with a major problem that she was having. The urge to help was immense and the fear of failing her friend bubbled from under the surface of her mind. She wanted to say yes but she could not help but think about how she let her client down and the disappointment she felt all day as a result. Tynika began deliberating with herself.

"If I tell her, "yes," and I go help, I will be completely drained afterward. I can't have another day like today but if I don't help she won't finish what she needs to finish and she will resent me. . . . Maybe resent is too harsh? Other friends can help her besides me. If she is a good friend she should understand, right? If I provide context about how rough my day was, she is sure to understand. Okay, that's it. I have to decline." Tynika explained everything, the whole time she felt as if she were betraying her friend.

Tynika was relieved when her friend replied and said that it was okay. She'd find someone else to help her. "It's that easy?" Tynika thought.

She was overextending herself for years, but the burden was all psychological. Tynika realized that she put unnecessary pressure on herself. She saw it as she was the only person who could help her friends because they came to her. She felt tasked with saving everyone. This helpful attitude was useful at her job but she needed to temper herself. The mental burden of it all had run her ragged. Thinking back, she realized that because of her experiences early on with the social worker who helped her family, that it was her duty to help everyone just like she was helped. It's just that she did not create any boundaries for herself. She didn't give her personal time and space enough value. Eventually, she came to terms with the overly helpful part of her personality and promised to treat herself better.

***

When others are routinely requesting our time, it is okay to say "no." We inflate the scenario in our minds and believe that if we don't say "yes" then the relationship will be jeopardized. We cannot always be there for everyone in our lives nor should we. Our day-to-day activities alone can be taxing. And if you do not carve out time for self-care, you are begging for burnout. We live in a society that worships the idea of overworking ourselves. Yet when we run ourselves ragged we are unable to perform well and no one wins. So take care of yourself, manage your workload, and regulate how much of yourself you give to others. You deserve better for yourself so you must create better for yourself.

Where the Money Reside

Affirmation: I am financially free.

"If I don't eat out for the next month and if I get a haircut every other week, I should be able to just make it," Dia considered. "Now I just need to do this for the next few months and I should have a decent amount saved . . . sorta." Dia was always calculating how much money he could save. His goal was to be rich someday. He wanted to have money in surplus so that he would not have to worry about anything. So he saved as much as he could and cut costs wherever possible.

However, he always felt like he wasn't doing enough or his efforts weren't good enough. He saved as much as possible for so long but in his opinion, he had not saved very much. He also would often dip into his savings to deal with different emergencies as they arose. His day-to-day was also very miserable because of all the cost-cutting he was doing. He was fed up with being poor and unsatisfied. Something had to give but he did not know what he was doing wrong. That evening he sat down with his young son to help him with questions for his math homework. The question read: If Jim makes $10 a day and spends $5 of that $10 daily, how many days will it take Jim to have $200. Dia chuckled at the simplicity of the question as he dropped little hints to help his son figure out the answer. He suddenly had a revelation.

"What does rich mean to me?" Dia wondered. How much was he supposed to save? How long should he save? They were questions he never considered until now. He just had it in his head that he wanted to be rich at all cost but never bothered to define it. So that's what he set out to do. He needed to define being rich. He sat down and thought of a figure that he wanted to aim for. That figure, he thought, would provide him a comfortable life. He would be able to do all the fun things he'd always dreamed of. He gave himself ten years to reach the amount. The only problem was that the number seemed way out of reach if he was only saving what he had left after expenses.

Dia knew that he needed more information. He needed to understand the financial world to know what he should be doing. He bought any book that he could get his hands on that dealt with finances, money, wealth, etc. He met with accountants, financial advisors, and insurance agents. He even attended a few seminars that spoke about money. He assumed that this would take him a few weeks but his journey developed into a five-month-long financial adventure, during which he spent a significant amount of money.

It was easy to get sucked in because the more he learned the more he realized what he did not know. One piece of financial information led to another and another and then another. He learned that up until this point, he'd been naive about his personal finances. With all the research he did over the past few months, Dia still did not have a solid grasp on his finances, but he did come to some new conclusions:

1. **He did not want to be rich but financially free**
2. **Saving alone would not make it happen**
3. **He needed specific financial goals**

He'd heard the term financially free many times during his financial education journey. He learned that it was about exiting the rat race, creating streams of passive income that were greater than his current expenses. He always felt like he was working endlessly but never had enough money. While his money resided in his savings, it did not work for him. He was not investing his money anywhere and therefore it was not growing. It was time for him to take action.

He worked with a financial advisor that he knew personally to come up with his new plan. He had to think long and hard about the specific targets he would aim for. It was tough for him to think long-term, but as he had a family to care for, he had extra motivation to do so. It was a laborious activity that required frequent sessions with the financial advisor. "The plan was pretty anti-climactic," he thought. On paper, it was a slow process that would take years and it wasn't very exciting. The money from his paycheck would be divided three different ways: savings, investments, and expenses. Looking at it all made him feel restless because it would take so long to reach his goals, but he knew the result would be worthwhile. The only way to speed up the plan would be to increase his income or start a side business. The latter option came with too much risk for Dia.

He thought of his family and began enacting the plan. Months went by, and even though the process was slow, he felt very accomplished that he was sticking with the plan. He loved checking on his different investments and slowly watching them grow. Eventually, he got to a point where he forgot about the investments that were still growing.

Before, he realized that he got caught up in the hype of what "rich" looks like. "Rich" was promoted as buying nice cars and mansions, flaunting your money on social media. But rich individuals are grinding, investing in themselves, and growing their money behind the scenes. Dia's money goals would take a while to obtain but he was confident that he would get there.

Five years later, Dia's investments had grown considerably. And he was able to earn a higher income at his job allowing him to put more money into his different investments. Because he had hit many of his targets, he planned to take the family on a lavish vacation to celebrate their success. Dia pledged to pass on all his valuable financial information to his son so that he will be properly prepared for a successful life.

***

Buzzwords like wealthy, rich, or financially free can be alluring. However, reaching the financial results that you want may require that you speak with an expert, or at the very least develop a plan on your own through self-education. You want to give yourself the best possible opportunities to hit your financial goals. The plan may be slow and boring but you trust in it and invest in yourself first. When your plan pays off in the end, you'll know that you've helped to create a better future for you and your family.

Don't Make Me Say "Manifestation"

Affirmation: I focus deeply on the things I want and then I go out and get them.

Day in and day out it was all the same for Ashonda. Life was okay but she was unsatisfied. Ashonda felt like there was more that she could be doing with her life. Although she mostly enjoyed her life, and she had a beautiful daughter, a decent job, still she couldn't help yearning for more. She just couldn't put her finger on what "more" was. She was a makeup artist during the day, working in a store at the mall. The store owner had a great deal of respect for her so Ashonda would run the store 90% of the time. Running the store was easy and she often felt bored.

On a typical day, many customers ran through the store. Ashonda's friends also took this as an opportunity to pop in from time to time to catch up with her. For one friend in particular, it was a daily ritual. He would visit with a nauseating frequency some weeks but Ashonda was happy for the company. During one of his visits, they talked about Ashonda's unsatisfied feelings. Her friend listened intently.

Then all of a sudden he yelled, "I have the secret." Ashonda rolled her eyes at his unnecessary eccentrics but played along. "What is the secret?" she asked. "*The Secret* is the secret," he replied. Ashonda grew impatient and reached out to tap him across his head. "Ouch!" he exclaimed. "Okay, okay," and he let out a loud chuckle. "It's a book about the law of attraction. It's a really popular book that's been around a long time. I am surprised you've never heard of it. There's an audio version I can loan to you. Take a listen during your free time."

Ashonda figured she had nothing to lose by taking her friend up on his offer. Some periods during the day were slow enough for her to listen to the audiobook. She agreed and her friend loaned her the recording. The next day Ashonda began listening to the audiobook. She was immediately turned off by the introductory music. It gave off a heavy hippy energy. But she did not let the introduction deter her and she listened on. The book spoke about all the different experts who contributed to making the book what it was. She, however, never heard of any of these people so she was not the least bit impressed. The narrator then mentioned the law of attraction and Ashonda's disbelief grew more and more as she listened.

She wondered, "What nonsense am I listening to?" She began questioning why she listened to her friend. The book spoke about attracting the things you want most for yourself by sending out positive energy into the "universe." She heard the word "manifesting" so many times that she thought she was reading a fiction book. The book was becoming more comic relief than anything else. As she listened on, she found herself constantly rolling her eyes at the unbelievable stories of people using simple thoughts to heal their severe illnesses and overcome their hardships. "What utter nonsense," she thought.

The stories all sounded far-fetched and absurd. "This stuff could never happen to me," she thought. The book gave scientific evidence to back up the claims but Ashonda was not biting. She then came to a story about a man who used the law of attraction to make 100,000 dollars. He simply stated his intention and left it for the universe to help him manifest it. Apparently, by leaving the door open to the possibility, he would eventually figure it out. In the story, the man did it by selling copies of his book "Chicken Soup for the Soul." "This has to be made up," she thought. She Googled the book and found that there were many versions of it and most, if not all, were bestsellers. Although she still could not fully accept what she was hearing, she figured there must be something to it and decided to run an experiment.

Following the method in the book, she pledged that she would double her earnings next year. She planned to make an additional $10,000 and put this law of attraction thing to the test. She would, however, not be using the words "manifestation" and "universe." Those terms were too offbeat for her liking. She began filling her thoughts with reaching her

177

target. She tried her best to fully believe that it would happen. It felt idiotic to her as she had no clue how she was going to make it a reality, but she persisted because this was what she wanted. She remembered one of the stories from the book where someone had a house on his vision board and eventually moved into the same house. Ashonda decided to do one better. She would download a picture of 10,000 dollars and place it as her wallpaper on her phone. She was always on her phone and she figured that would have a greater effect than a vision board.

Each day the idea of making $10,000 drilled deeper and deeper into her mind, to the point where she would think about it without looking at her phone. She assumed the "law of attraction" would start kicking in soon. One day, a frequent customer of Ashonda's was getting her makeup done and mentioned that her best friend was getting married soon and that the wedding dress looked amazing. Ashonda then asked, "Who is doing the makeup for the bride and bridesmaids?" The woman answered, "I'm not sure but you should do it! I always come here to get my makeup done and you do an excellent job. I will talk to her about it."

Just like that, Ashonda had her first makeup gig. By no means was it easy. She had to arrive early that morning and there were seven bridesmaids plus the bride. The women loved her work. By the time she was done, Ashonda had made a sizable amount of money. She realized that booking makeup gigs were a no-brainer. She should keep doing makeup after work to make up the $10,000. She couldn't believe she never thought of this.

Ashonda began doing makeup for weddings, for women before they went to parties, and for her friends on weekends. She created a social media page which helped to increase her exposure. Her boss noticed what she was doing and offered to sponsor some product from the store once she mentioned it to her clients. Ashonda agreed. It was all going way too well. As the weeks passed, she amassed more and more regular clients to the point where she would work well into the night some days with no rest. Two weeks before the year was about to end Ashonda had made $8,650. Although she was a bit short of her $10,000 target it was still an astonishing achievement.

Ashonda had a taste of the possibilities and began setting her intentions for what the next year would look like. She included what she wanted in all the areas of her life. "If this could work for money, it could work for anything," she thought. She still would not be caught dead using the word "manifestation." Nevertheless, she saw the merit in affirming what she wanted for herself and allowing for the possibilities to take shape.

***

The law of attraction can appear to be more science fiction than reality, but it works. When you focus on what you want for yourself deeply and intensely on a daily basis, you will eventually figure out how to make it a reality. Your goals, however, do not just fall into your lap. The pieces will be shown to you and it's up to you to put those pieces together. Some call it the universe and some say it's God providing for us. Whatever you believe, it starts with you stating your intentions and truly believing that it will become a reality.

Acknowledgments

I would like to thank all the many people that inspired the stories within this book. Thanks go out to Azariel Pedro (Twitter: @azarie_), Kristoff Alexander, Janel Phillip, Darcelle Wilson, Nechelle Achong, Ajala Pilgrim, Jeremiah Lyndon, Andrea Bernard, Valerie Dhandoolal, Saran and Devon Fournillier from KrumbsTT (IG: Krumbstt), Fayola Fraser, Alexander Fraser, Kerron Hyndman from Swagg Elite artistry (IG: swagg_elite_vanguard), Sabrina Mohammed, Sarah Drepaul, Kayla Bostic (Tik Tok: @kaylabostic4), Justin Seheult (IG: _financialguide), Nkese P (IG: nkesepofficial), Brittany Leotaud, the members of the Rotaract Club of Port of Spain West (IG: rotaractposwest), Tynika James, Jarrod Best-Mitchell and Ashonda James (IG: makeupbyshon91). Special thanks to Gionieva Fraser for helping me chose a name for this book.

Thanks also to all my friends and family whose names are scattered amongst the characters in the stories. Most importantly I want to thank everyone that decided to read this book. Especially, if you read my first book The Millennial Mind and picked up this book, thank you very much! None of this would be possible without you.

I hope the stories in this book motivate you to make the little changes in your life that will have a big impact. Your potential is only caged by what you believe is possible so dream big and work hard towards your goals.

You've made it this far. I'd love to know what you thought about my book and the information therein. For free resources, connect with me by email at themillennialmind2020@gmail.com and visit my website www.rebityouth.com.

www.ingramcontent.com/pod-product-compliance
Lightning Source LLC
Chambersburg PA
CBHW072122170626
46813CB00004B/1655